MW00942830

Mystical Aria:
Seeking the Gallion Queen

Mystical Aria:
Seeking the
Gallion Queen

Jean Neff Guthrie

To: McKenzie
Live Peace!

Jean Neff Guthrie

Copyright © 2015 by Jean Neff Guthrie

All rights reserved.

Book design by Jean Neff Guthrie

Cover design by Michele Phillips Illustration

This is a work of fiction. Names, characters, businesses, places, and events are either the products of the author's imagination or are used in a fictitious manner. Any resemblance to actual persons, living or dead, or actual events is purely coincidental.

No part of this book may be reproduced or transmitted in any form or by any means, electronic or mechanical, including photocopying, recording, or any information storage and retrieval systems, without permission in writing from the author.

Jean Neff Guthrie Books are available for order through Ingram Press Catalogs

Visit my website at http://JeanNeffGuthrie.com

Printed in the United States of America

First Printing: December 2015

Published by Sojourn Publishing, LLC

ISBN: 978-1-62747-161-9
Ebook ISBN: 978-1-62747-162-6

Dedicated to my family
Dad, Mom, Ellen, and Joe

But if we decide that the universe is a friendly place, then we will use our technology, our scientific discoveries and our natural resources to create tools and models for understanding that universe. Because power and safety will come through understanding its workings and its motives.
–Albert Einstein

Somewhere, something incredible is waiting to be known.
–Carl Sagan

Acknowledgments

My novel would have festered inside me if I hadn't met my writing mentor, Tom Bird. From attending one of his writing courses at Emory University in Atlanta, Georgia, to speaking with him daily about my writing progress, Tom has helped me ground my sci-fi imagination into a voice that entertains and inspires young readers.

I first heard the voice of Aria Vanir while attending a media training retreat conducted by Tom and David Thalberg, Founding Partner at BrandStand. I credit them with creating a safe environment to go deep within and release this amazing character.

My nieces and nephews kept me inspired during years of editing. The look of attention in their eyes while reading them early manuscripts helped me believe that the hours and hours to improve this novel were absolutely worthwhile.

Copyeditor, Liliane McCarthy, and teen development editor, Daren Fowler, raised the bar on the quality of my writing. Michele Phillips, illustrator, brought to life my vision of Aria and an exquisite alien queen.

My English teachers, from elementary school through college, could never receive enough appreciation for encouraging and instructing me.

I also acknowledge my mother for instilling a fondness for good literature. As a kid, her constant corrections of my grammar annoyed me. As an adult, I am thankful.

A few years before he died, I was talking with my father about taking the next step to publishing my book. How important this was to me. Usually not the outwardly encouraging one, he surprised me with three words I will remember for the rest of my life: "Go do it."

Characters on Vitchera

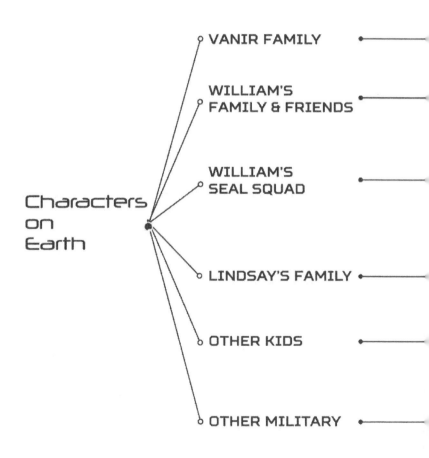

GALLIONS

Characters on Earth

VANIR FAMILY

WILLIAM'S FAMILY & FRIENDS

WILLIAM'S SEAL SQUAD

LINDSAY'S FAMILY

OTHER KIDS

OTHER MILITARY

- Queen Supreme Nashata
- Mitushi - Commander Supreme
- Princess LeliaSomona (LeSom)
- Orakakima (Ora) - Ambassador Supreme
- Peakte - First Engineer
- Arcthena - Security Handmaiden
- Forkana - Hospitality Handmaiden
- Marta - First Teleporter
- Gauzette - First Healer
- PomPass - First Navigator
- Butch - First Invader
- Shemuse - Unicorn

- Aria
- Jackie - sister
- Lindsay - mother
- William - father

- Colonel Jackson Vanir - William's father
- Mrs. Hale
- Jeremy Hale

- Lieutenant Elizabeth "Saltine" Manger - Tommy's mother
- Lieutenant Commander Christopher "Dishtowel" Ragg
- Hammer
- Mars
- Ringer
- Toothpick
- Tumbleweed

- Fancy Mae Hiddleman - Aria's grandmother
- Summer Dae Perrier
- Elizabeth Kate Lee
- Jacqueline Anna Valentine

- Tommy Manger - Aria's BFF
- Drake Manger - Tommy's brother
- Meredith Spheeris - Aria's friend
- Eric Watts - bully

- Vice Admiral Albert Jennings
- General Peter Goforth
- Lieutenant Dewey
- Ensign Jacob "Headrock" Marshall

Chapter 1
The Call

Aria Vanir breezed through her seventh-grade homework to focus on far more important matters. While many of her friends and neighbors gathered at the Virginia Beach boardwalk to admire the amber and ruby rays from the setting sun, Aria preferred to gaze through her bedroom window at the darkening heavens. For her, twilight welcomed the dawn of the stars. On this clear evening in late May 2028, Aria mindlessly tapped her fingers against the top of her transmission binder, or tBinder, as she wondered who lived among those twinkling orbs.

Aria's mother, Lindsay, came into the bedroom and asked to see her homework. With a smile on her face, Aria handed her tBinder to her mother. Lindsay knew from Aria's happy expression that all the answers probably were correct. Still, Virginia Beach's North End schools had asked one parent or guardian to check homework every night. Lindsay sat at Aria's Hospitality Station—with its three chairs and a small table for serving tea—and opened the tBinder.

Over the past five years, tBinders had replaced books and electronic devices in schools. Teachers now downloaded lessons, documentaries, homework assignments, and tests into their students' tBinders. Parents or guardians checked homework against an answer section that was protected with a fingerprint tScan. Then the students uploaded their assignments to their teachers' tBinders, which automatically graded homework, quizzes, and tests.

As Lindsay scanned the tBinder files, Aria pulled back her long auburn hair into a thick ponytail and practiced ballet steps by the edge of her bed. Aria's slender body and flexible limbs made even the more challenging moves look effortless. For Aria, dancing was the one thing that put her busy mind at rest. Although she was one of the smallest girls in her ballet class, as well as in the seventh grade, she often was selected for starring roles in recitals.

"Your homework looks great, honey," Lindsay said as she pressed *Back* to go to the beginning of the assignment. Like Aria, she had bony fingers and a dainty frame. They definitely looked like a mother-daughter pair, except Lindsay was a brunette with green eyes. Aria had inherited her father's blue eyes and fair skin. Lindsay clicked *Tools - Signature*, and the tBinder automatically generated her electronic signature to indicate her approval of Aria's homework. "I especially like your description of Thomas Jefferson's home. Excellent detail."

"Thanks, Mom," Aria replied as she raised her hands over her head into third position. Aria recalled everything from her school trip to Monticello in Charlottesville, Virginia. For that matter, she remembered everything she had ever seen, from words and equations on her tBinder to license plates and paintings. Aria rarely needed to study. She just saw the answers in front of her face whenever a teacher asked her a question or she was taking a test. To Aria, this photographic memory was perfectly natural.

Lindsay started to leave, but Aria wanted to tell her mother about her latest psychic impression. Aria confided only in her mother about these visions of future events, yet giving voice to them still made Aria anxious. She needed some quiet time with her mom to ease into telling her about Mrs. Higgins.

"Wait, Mom. Would you like to stay for a cup of tea? I can make decaf since it's after supper." Aria picked up a box of chamomile with lavender tea from her Hospitality Station and waved it in the air. She knew how much her mother enjoyed drinking calming tea in the evenings.

Although Lindsay was quite busy that evening, she didn't have the heart to say no. She poured filtered hot water from the kitchen sink into two mugs and brought them to Aria's bedroom.

Since she had been a little girl, Aria's favorite hobby was hosting tea parties. Her parents said she had picked it up from her Grandma Hiddleman, who had served tea in her mansion every Saturday afternoon at three o'clock. After Aria had read a sign that said "Hospitality Station" at a self-serve breakfast bar in a hotel, she had insisted that the table and chairs used for her tea parties be called her Hospitality Station.

While Aria prepared the tea, Lindsay asked, "Mind if I put on some music?" Aria rolled her eyes to the ceiling because she knew her mom would want to play that classical stuff. Yuck. However, Aria also noticed that her mother smiled more and even swayed when she heard the tunes of Bach, Chopin, and Mozart. To keep her mom happy, she nodded in agreement.

Lindsay pressed a few buttons on her watch, which started a mix of Bach's greatest hits. The first piece was a favorite she often had played as a stressed-out mother with a toddler, Jackie, a baby on the way, and a husband somewhere overseas. It had soothed her nerves. Lindsay rubbed her belly as she had when pregnant with Aria.

"Did I ever tell you—" Lindsay started.

Aria knew where this was going and interrupted, "Yeah, yeah, yeah, that you wanted to name me Aria after your favorite Bach song." Aria handed her mother a mug of herbal tea and added, "You've told me an astro zillion times, Mom."

Lindsay confided, "The toughest part about giving birth to you was not knowing where your father was. I prayed every morning that he was alive and safe. When you were a few days old, I was allowed a short tView for the three of us. You were crying at first but stopped as soon as you heard his voice. Then you stared intently into the tViewer at this handsome SEAL and giggled, like you already knew him."

Aria asked questions about her father's life when she was a baby and toddler. Lindsay told her what she knew, which wasn't much because his frequent missions were top secret. As Lindsay drank the last sip of her tea, she quietly gave thanks that her family was finally under one roof. Even if just for tonight.

"Now I have to check your sister's homework," Lindsay said as she started to leave Aria's bedroom. Aria grabbed her mother's arm before she reached the door.

"Mom," Aria exclaimed in a frantic voice. "Please check on Mrs. Higgins tomorrow evening."

With a puzzled look on her face, Lindsay asked, "Why, dear?"

Aria mumbled, "Just because . . . you know . . . she may be hurt after the fall she'll have tomorrow." Aria released her grip on her mother's arm and turned around.

"Okay," Lindsay whispered. Based on Aria's accurate predictions, Lindsay had learned to trust her daughter's guidance. As Lindsay left Aria's bedroom, she recalled the first time she had acknowledged that her daughter possessed unusual abilities.

Lindsay and Aria had been shopping in the grocery store. Aria, barely three years old at the time, had stared at a young man as he had been picking out two bunches of broccoli. As they had left the produce section, Aria had waved to him and yelled, "Bye-bye, Mr. Fireman!" When they had arrived home, Lindsay had told Aria not to yell at strangers anymore. Aria had apologized, and then she had rambled on and on about seeing pictures in the air of this man fighting fires. That was her way of explaining her multidimensional psychic impressions with her limited vocabulary. Lindsay just shook her head and told Aria to forget about it. This had been Lindsay's customary reaction whenever Aria had told her something was about to happen to a neighbor or someone she had just met.

The following week, Lindsay and Aria had seen that same young man at the post office. Again, Aria had waved at him. She had opened her mouth to shout at him again, so Lindsay had placed her finger on Aria's lips to keep her quiet. Lindsay then apologized to him for Aria's outburst at the grocery store. The young man had smiled and winked at Aria. He explained he was scheduled to start firefighter training two days after he had met them in the grocery store. He had been having doubts about his decision, but Aria's greeting inspired him. He said it had given him the courage to endure the most demanding physical challenge of his life.

Lindsay had felt scared when she realized that Aria possessed psychic talents. Yet she instinctively knew she needed to love her daughter and understand what was going on inside her head. Lindsay had decided to learn more about Aria's impressions without anyone else knowing. She didn't want Aria committed to an institution or studied by the government. Every afternoon, when the two of them were alone, Lindsay had asked Aria about the people they had met that day. Lindsay had written down everything Aria said about what would happen to whom. Much to Lindsay's surprise, over ninety percent of Aria's predictions had come true.

Lindsay had strongly warned Aria not to speak of her impressions to anyone else. Since they were so close, Aria had trusted her mother's guidance. As she went through elementary school, Aria had noticed that unique kids with special gifts often were teased by the other children. Aria had wanted to fit in and be accepted by her peers, so she had kept her psychic talents a secret from everyone—except her mother.

After leaving Aria's bedroom, Lindsay went down the hall and knocked on her older daughter's door.

"Jacqueline, dear, I need to check your homework," Lindsay said as she walked into the bedroom. As Jackie completed a spinning crescent kick, her foot almost hit her mother's face. Lindsay knew the near-miss was an accident, but she frowned at her daughter anyway. "The tBinder, please."

Fifteen-year-old Jacqueline cared as much for school and homework as cats do for swimming. They just didn't mix. With the gladiator body frame she had inherited from her dad, Jackie was one of the largest and most athletic girls at North End High School. She kept her blonde hair cut above her shoulders. That way her wavy locks never bothered her when she played sports, which was one of her two passions. Jackie's other ambition was fighting the enemy, just like Dad.

"Nuke the tBinder!" Jackie exclaimed. "Can't you see I'm practicing my kata? Regional competitions are in two weeks, and my form must be astro perfect." Jackie flung her bo—a six-foot stick used in Japanese martial arts—around her waist and then in front of her. She pretended her mother was a judge in the final round of the Mid-Atlantic Regional Karate Competition. "How did that look, Mom?"

Lindsay shook her head and put her hands on her waist. Two shelves of trophies and ribbons in the far corner caught Lindsay's attention. Jackie had won them in sporting events wherever the family had lived. Karate in Japan, soccer in Germany, and softball in the United States. Competition—whether alone or part of a team—gave Jackie a way to express herself and make friends quickly.

With a strict tone, Lindsay demanded, "Your homework, Jacqueline."

"I told you, Mom," Jackie replied in a sarcastic tone, "my kata!" She stepped back and quickly moved her bo from side to side, which was another required form.

Lindsay stormed out of Jackie's bedroom and slammed the door behind her. For years they had fought over this issue of homework versus sports. Again, Lindsay resorted to the one method that had proved effective with Jackie.

"William!" Lindsay shouted as she marched down the hall and into the living room. Aria giggled when she heard her mother yell. She knew Jackie was in for it now.

William Vanir was relaxing in his recliner and watching the baseball game on tHTV. Holographic TV technology had replaced high definition years ago. It transmitted three-dimensional images of the players into the room so he had a greater sense of actually being at the game.

Lindsay walked to William's side and explained, "It's *your* daughter." The way she said it alerted William that Jacqueline needed more discipline.

William and Lindsay had joked about Jackie being Daddy's girl since she was a toddler. She looked like him—sunshine hair, sandy skin, ocean eyes, a lifeguard build, and bumps in the middle of their noses. She imitated the way he walked, with square shoulders and head held high. Instead of playing with dolls, she pretended to gather intel from behind enemy lines.

William secretly had wished for a son as his firstborn child to pass down his military lineage. From present-day terrorist attacks on American soil back to the Revolutionary War, Vanir men had fought bravely to save their families and country. In case Jackie wanted to join the military, William encouraged her interests in martial arts and team sports. However, not at the expense of her education.

William jumped out of his recliner, turned off the tHTV, and told Lindsay he'd take care of it—again. He walked into Jackie's room without knocking.

With a gruff voice he blared, "Jack, put down the bo and do your homework." William called his older daughter Jack, partly to encourage her tomboy nature. Lindsay called her Jacqueline in honor of her favorite aunt, who had been named after Jacqueline Kennedy Onassis. Aria, the kids at school, and almost everyone else just called her Jackie.

Jackie was in a feisty mood and wanted to test the boundaries with her father. She continued to practice her moves as though her father had never entered the bedroom.

William puffed up his chest and loudly exclaimed, "No more kata, Jack. Take off the black belt, put down the bo, and open the tBinder. Now!" Jackie didn't move. William stepped up to her and yelled, "Go, go, go!"

The Vanir girls knew what "go, go, go" meant long before they had watched their first action film. It meant get a move on and do what Dad said or else.

Jackie immediately stopped her karate and started her homework. William didn't enjoy yelling at Jack, but he knew that discipline turned slackers into first-rate sailors.

"Jack, you need to make good grades in science and math," William insisted. "Cadets must master calculus to even think about being in the space program. I'll check your homework again tomorrow night. And the next."

When Aria heard her father mention the space program, she again surveyed the night sky. By now the horizon was dark with dozens of twinkling stars. Aria squinted to find the smallest star far, far away. There it was, a pinkish-white speck in the east.

"Astro," Aria whispered to herself. "I wonder if there's anyone else like me, Mom, Dad, and Jackie out there. Like, nice alien families. Surely there must be good aliens who want to visit Earth and meet humans." Aria leaned closer to her window and searched deeply into space. The vastness of the night sky mesmerized her.

Aria felt an eerie sensation in her body, which happened every time she received predictions. Then, images of a planet with two suns appeared in the air. Beside them emerged pictures of rounded mountains with no trees and cream-colored oceans filled with small waves. In another scene, large black birds dived into the water and swam like fish.

"Funtastic!" Aria said softly so no one would hear her. She wanted to keep these visions a secret, especially since they were about another world—possibly another galaxy! The images disappeared as quickly as they had come into sight. "Wait, come back!" Aria pleaded. She knew, however, that her impressions lasted just long enough for her to get the message. But what were these visions telling her?

Aria's first hunch was that aliens on this distant planet wanted to visit her in Virginia Beach. Could this be true? Could she be part of an intergalactic foreign-exchange program? Could she become the youngest ambassador to seek peaceful relationships with extraterrestrials?

Aria felt so excited. She clapped her hands together and squealed. She *so* wanted to share what had happened with someone, but she feared that not even her mother was ready for this. Aria assumed her mom would go nuclear. She quickly sat at her desk and opened the tDiary that her parents had given her for Christmas. With this technology, she could type on a small keyboard or write on an electronic pad with a tPen. Aria felt more connected with the words when she wrote, so she preferred to use the tPen.

> *Monday, May 22, 2028*
>
> *Calling all aliens! Hi. My name is Aria. I'm 12 years old and live in Virginia Beach. That's in Virginia, which is in the United States. That's in North America, which is on the top part of Earth. I am in the seventh grade at Virginia Beach Middle School. I take ballet lessons after school and like history class the best.*
>
> *Friday was my birthday, so really I'm 12 years and 3 days old. I got games and ballet slippers and clothes for my birthday. My friend Tommy—he's just a friend and we aren't going together—gave*

me the latest Galactic Gina *book. We both like stories and movies about spaceships.*

Would you like to travel to Earth in your spaceship and visit me? School ends in a few weeks, and we could hang out at the beach every day. Except when it rains. Tommy and I build sandcastles. My sister, Jackie, and her friends surf whenever the waves are high enough. Summer is a really funtastic time, especially since I don't have any homework.

You can stay at our house. Mom fixes up the guest room with fresh flowers whenever we have visitors. It always smells sweet, especially when she cuts jasmine or roses from the yard. And we always eat fresh seafood when we have company.

I'm sure you'll be happy here, especially the aliens from the planet with 2 suns and small, treeless mountains and black birds that swim and . . . oh yeah, small waves in a white ocean. We have bigger waves on blue waters, and our birds have to stay in the air or float on the water. Otherwise they'd drown. Jackie couldn't surf on your planet. We would have fun in a raft, though.

Well, that's all I have to say right now. Ask your parents if you can visit me. Good night.

Your ambassador from Earth,
Aria Vanir.

Aria pressed her thumb on the tScan and wrote her secret password. The tDiary saved her written text to a file. Aria closed the top of her tDiary and wondered if anyone would get her message.

Chapter 2
The Gallions

On the planet Vitchera, three galaxies from Earth, a petite unicorn named Shemuse galloped across a blue meadow that bordered a milky ocean. Two suns appeared to rise on opposite ends of the horizon, one in the east and the other west. The unicorn startled the aquards, large birds with black feathers, as they sat on the banks of the water. The aquards flew into the air and then dived into the water. Their beaks had a secondary function as gills, which allowed them to swim for twenty minutes. The erratic flight patterns of the aquards didn't bother Shemuse, who hastily continued her journey to the land of the Gallions.

The Gallions had evolved golden, glassy skin that protected them by reflecting the intense rays from two suns. Their large, lavender eyes absorbed a tremendous amount of light. Gallions walked upright like humans, with exceptionally strong legs and an average height of six feet. Unlike humans, they had whiskers on top of their heads instead of hair. They grew tentacles in place of arms. The ends of their tentacles divided into eight tips, like fingers. The tentacles were normally as long as human arms, but the Gallions could stretch them to nearly nine feet. It made fetching things quite easy.

Gallions recognized each other by black markings on their bodies. A series of stripes, ellipses, and circles on their backs indicated their tribe origination. More sophisticated stars, spheres, and spirals on their chests told who they were within their families.

The Gallions lived in gigantic, circular homes of rock. The top halves of their homes were above the ground. The bottom parts reached into an aquifer that fed the nearby ocean. The complete village resembled bunches of supersized hornets' nests. Since only the top halves of the homes were visible, they simply looked like small mountains without any trees or bushes.

When Shemuse reached the land of the Gallions, she followed a narrow path between the rounded stone homes until she reached the center of the village. There, she entered the palace of Queen Supreme Nashata, Galactic Mother of the Gallions.

Unicorns on Vitchera possessed highly evolved, gold horns that sent and received intergalactic messages. The Gallions had nicknamed them communicorns. Shemuse had the longest, brightest horn of all the communicorns. She had been in contact with aliens from five galaxies away, a planetary record for her species. The queen wanted the best for her royal court, so she had asked Shemuse to serve as her official communicorn.

Protectors for the queen swiftly escorted Shemuse to the Central Quarter, where the Gallion royal family conducted its business. The protectors moved quickly and cautiously because visits from this particular animal were vital to the queen—and the rest of the Gallions. Shemuse pranced to Queen Supreme Nashata, who sat on her throne, and bowed in front of her.

Then Shemuse straightened up and said, "Your Majesty, you have a call. From Earth. The Atlantic Quadrant, to be exact."

The queen's lavender eyes widened as she replied, "The Atlantic Quadrant of Earth, you say?"

"Precisely, Your Majesty. The Atlantic Quadrant."

"Must be Washington again," the queen responded with a harsh tone. Prior observations and attempted contacts had taught her not to trust governments on Earth. "FBI, CIA, X-Files? Those bureaucrats are always sending messages of peace and hope. But look at what the hypocrites did at Roswell!"

"Not Washington, Your Majesty."

"United Nations? Secret Service? Homeland Security?"

The Gallions had intercepted messages from these organizations as well. The queen, an intelligent yet cautious Gallion leader, had decided not to communicate with them at this point. Instead she wanted to observe them until humans had evolved to a more hospitable state of being.

"Not exactly, Your Majesty." Then Shemuse paused. She hardly believed the source of the call herself and hesitated to inform the royal family. Still, it was her duty. "From . . . er, ah . . . Virginia Beach."

"Ah, Virginia Beach," Queen Supreme Nashata replied with a softer tone. The news made her feel hopeful, causing the whiskers on top of her head to form a U. "So the underwater satellites of Atlantis must be operational again."

"Not exactly, Your Majesty." Shemuse knew how much the queen enjoyed guessing the source of her messages to show her extensive knowledge of alien worlds. The communicorn assumed, however, she'd never guess this unique sender. Shemuse finally blurted, "The call came from the tDiary of a human youngirl, Aria Vanir."

"A youngirl!" Queen Supreme Nashata exclaimed. Her whiskers spiked from the excitement. "A youngirl used primitive technology to send an intergalactic message. Splendid!"

"Not only that, Your Majesty, but she mentions a world like ours. I believe she has seen Vitchera. Would you like to hear the message?"

"Yes, yes, of course!" the queen exclaimed. She quickly stretched one of her tentacles until it touched the tip of Shemuse's golden horn.

A holographic image of Aria writing in her tDiary appeared. The past two generations of communicorns had advanced to show video of the sender as well as audio of the message. Queen Supreme Nashata listened to Aria's call. Her whiskers parted into a U when she received the invitation to visit Aria and go to the beach. She thought that was sweet, even though she knew her presence there would send the world into a panic.

When Aria perfectly described the land of the Gallions, the queen's whiskers spiked again. The queen asked Shemuse to replay that part three times. Her whiskers flowed side to side as she contemplated the revelation

How could a human youngirl on Earth, the queen wondered, *know so much about the land of the Gallions? Of all the aliens, why would Aria specifically invite the Gallions to visit her? Could this be the sign I've been waiting for?*

The queen sat upright with pointed whiskers and demanded, "Get Mitushi on the horn at once!"

Shemuse blinked her eyes and switched her tail to help reset the holographic monitor in her horn. A new image appeared of Mitushi, commander supreme of the Gallion Fleet and son of the queen. He and twelve of his captains were studying star maps and discussing their upcoming voyages.

The Gallions prided themselves on being peaceful explorers who observed other life-forms with the intent to connect, not dominate. They believed that the One Provider created all life in divine harmony, and so all life-forms should live that way. Certainly, other worlds had attempted to capture the Gallions, destroy their land, or even blow up the entire planet of Vitchera. With their superior technology and skillful sneakiness, the Gallions—under the leadership of Mitushi and his ancestors—had thwarted all enemies during the past three thousand years. Needless to say, the Gallions loved and admired Mitushi.

"Mitushi!" the queen blared. Mitushi heard his mother's voice above his whiskers. For that matter, all twelve captains acknowledged Her Majesty's voice by standing at attention.

Mitushi raised his left tentacle tips to his eyes and stated, "Mitushi, present and ready to receive signal."

Shemuse recognized Mitushi's one-of-a-kind voiceprint and opened a channel between him and the queen. An image of the queen appeared on Mitushi's left tentacle.

"Son, I need to speak with you about a new mission," Queen Supreme Nashata explained. She lowered her voice and added, "Privately." The twelve captains departed without a word.

"We're alone now, Mother. But I can tell you that all our captains are busy with high-priority assignments we've already given them."

The queen blared, "I don't want any of our captains for this mission, Mitushi. I want you! This will be a long voyage, and I want a safe, smooth ride. You know how turbulence splits my whiskers."

"You want to fly on a mission?" Mitushi inquired for clarification. His whiskers flowed side to side as he tried to remember the last time his mother had flown into battle or on a diplomatic assignment. Usually she preferred to stay on Vitchera and observe people, plants, and planets in the Gallery of Worlds.

The Gallery of Worlds was a library in the royal home. It contained all the messages received and sent by the communicorns. Lately they had been updated to holographic audio and video so the queen could easily see and hear about life on thousands of planets. She simply stated the name of the land or world, and images of that area appeared in the center of the Gallery. She could zoom in or out, fast forward, and rewind to find the information she wanted. Sometimes the queen asked Shemuse to open a portal of silence to a strange planet. This allowed the queen to observe alien life-forms secretly before deciding if she wanted to contact them.

"Where do you want to go?" Mitushi asked. "And why?"

"To Earth!" Queen Supreme Nashata exclaimed. "We've been invited—"

"Earth?" Princess LeliaSomona squealed as she entered the Central Quarter and interrupted her older sister. "As in Elvis?"

Princess LeliaSomona—LeSom for short—had the most refined whiskers of any Gallion. They enabled her to imitate whatever she had heard, from complicated dialects to space-age music. She had used the Gallery of Worlds to learn songs and languages of all known planets. Her favorite Earth musician of all time was, of course, Elvis Presley.

"Yes, and you are late for your royal appointments. Sit on your throne *quietly* until I finish my message to Mitushi."

"I want to go to Earth," Princess LeSom pleaded as she walked across the stone floor to her throne. "We can visit Elvis Presley's home, Graceland." Princess LeSom's whiskers curled in front to mimic the rock star's hair. In her best Elvis voice, she sang, "You ain't nothin' but a hound dog!"

Queen Supreme Nashata interrupted, "Quietly means quietly!"

The queen's harsh tone upset Princess LeSom, causing her whiskers to droop to the side of her face. She sulked in her throne and again wished she had been born first.

The queen calmed down and then told Mitushi about the call from youngirl Aria Vanir. Mitushi knew his mother had studied people from thousands of planets and carefully had selected the ones she wanted to call friends. He also remembered how his mother had told him to stay away from the humans until just the right time. Evidently that moment had arrived.

"I've waited my whole life for peaceful contact with Earth humans," the queen explained. "I want everything to go smoothly for this diplomatic adventure. Mitushi, prepare your finest superspaceship and crew. LeSom, brush up on the terms American youngirls use these days. I may need you to interpret slang." Princess LeSom's whiskers spiked when she realized she might see Graceland. "Oh, and Mitushi, bring your wife and four of her best shielders. Just in case we experience . . . resistance."

Chapter 3
The Great Tea Initiation

The following Saturday, William and his daughters gathered at Aria's Hospitality Station for the Vanir's traditional three o'clock tea party. Lindsay had asked William to cover for both of them because she had promised to spend the afternoon helping Mrs. Higgins, who had broken her wrist during a fall earlier that week. William smiled and hummed as he poured tea for his daughters. Jackie wanted to know why he was so happy and comfortable doing something that didn't involve spies or a covert operation. William laughed and explained that tea always reminded him of how he had met their mother. Jackie and Aria begged their father to give them more details—what happened, where they met, whether they kissed, and what they thought of each other. William took a deep breath and two sips of tea before telling his story of the Great Tea Initiation.

William's father, Colonel Jackson Vanir, wanted his son to attend the best high school in Virginia to prepare him for college at Virginia Military Institute. When he requested and received a senior position with the CIA, Jackson moved his family— his wife and fifteen-year-old William—from a military base in California to the wealthy suburb of McLean, Virginia. He bought the only home he could afford in McClean's best neighborhood, a small ranch with broken windows and leaky pipes.

Girls flocked around William, the hot hunk from California. William noticed only Lindsay Hiddleman, the cute brunette known for her painting, dancing, debating, and trust funds. Unfortunately, he believed she was totally out of his league.

Lindsay's father owned several local banks. Her mother's family, from Louisiana, drilled oil in the Gulf of Mexico. The Hiddlemans lived in one of the largest houses in McLean, a red brick mansion on a hill overlooking a golf course. The home was protected with a black iron fence and a security gate.

William made it a point to pass Lindsay's house every time he went jogging or ran errands. He discovered that Lindsay walked her gray cat, Mittens, after school and twice on the weekends. William timed his runs on the sidewalk by the Hiddleman home as Lindsay strolled with Mittens on the grounds. They waved at each other, but the large iron fence always separated them.

On the weekends, William watched the security gate open for young men with fancy sports cars. He assumed they were there to date Lindsay, which was true. William knew he wasn't the rich country-club type and doubted he'd fit in with the Hiddleman family. Despite his desire to get to know Lindsay, he never asked her out on a date.

William entered Virginia Military Institute when Lindsay was still a junior in high school. At home from VMI for Thanksgiving break, he jogged every day near Lindsay's home when she normally walked Mittens.

This particular day, William heard screams and cries for help when he was a block from Lindsay's home. He recognized her voice and panicked. William sprinted in the direction of Lindsay's screams and saw two strange guys chasing her up the hill.

Ten minutes earlier, three juvenile delinquents from the inner city had been driving through the neighborhood. They had been checking out wealthy homes vacated for the holidays as their next heist. When they had driven past the Hiddleman home, they had whistled at Lindsay and had yelled obscenities at her. Lindsay had ignored the delinquents, which only angered them. High on the latest drug, MacMacho, they became even more obnoxious and threatened Lindsay.

Fed up, Lindsay had given them the finger and yelled, "Shut up, you jerks!" The delinquents, overly influenced by MacMacho, had decided to make an example of this vindictive rich girl.

The delinquents had stopped their car and had stormed the fence. One of them had hoisted the other two over the tall rails. Lindsay had grabbed Mittens, who was due in a few weeks to give birth to her first litter, and had started running to the house. She had screamed at the top of her lungs, which thankfully had alerted William.

When William reached the Hiddleman property, he quickly climbed over the iron fence. It was a breeze compared to the walls he had scaled while running obstacle courses at VMI. William chased the delinquents until he tackled one to the ground.

"Keep running," he yelled to Lindsay.

As William raised his hand to punch the guy under him, the second delinquent pulled a knife and cut William's right arm. William sprang to his feet to avoid another hit and to assess his opponents. In a split second, William's high school wrestling and VMI combat training pulled together in his psyche. William grabbed the guy who had cut him, flipped him onto his back, and took the knife. William kicked the second guy three times—once in the chest and twice in the gut. Both delinquents were now on their backs, moaning. The third, still on the other side of the fence, ran to the car. As he peeled out in a cloud of smoke, William squinted to read the license plate and commit it to memory.

William bound the delinquents' hands and feet with their shoelaces and stuffed their stinky socks into their mouths. He ran to the Hiddleman home to check on Lindsay. With the rush of adrenaline still pumping through his veins, it never occurred to him to feel inferior about his status in society. He just wanted to ensure Lindsay was safe.

Lindsay dashed out of the house, holding a plush cat carrier with Mittens in it. Tears streamed down her face. She frantically told William that Mittens had passed out, and she feared for the unborn kittens. William told her that he'd drive them in her car to the emergency veterinarian clinic.

An hour later, the vet told Lindsay that Mittens had given birth to three tiny kittens. He explained they needed special care for a month, but they should grow up to be as healthy as Mittens. On the way back to Lindsay's home, William and Lindsay talked about names for the kittens as though they had been friends for years. Lindsay named a gray kitten Gloves because it looked just like its mother. She called the other one, a black kitten with white paws, Boots. William named the yellow-and-white-striped one Boxer, short for Boxer Shorts. By the time they reached the mansion, Lindsay was laughing about the whole ordeal.

At the mansion, Lindsay and William described what had happened to a policeman who had arrested the delinquents. As they talked, another policeman bandaged William's arm.

After the police left, Lindsay introduced William to her parents. They thanked William and said they felt delighted to have such a brave neighbor. Lindsay's mother, Fancy Mae, insisted that William join her family for tea that Saturday afternoon, promptly at three o'clock. William looked at Lindsay, who was smiling ear-to-ear. He accepted, hoping to spend more time with the girl of his dreams.

Unknown to William, Fancy Mae had made every boy who had ever wanted to date Lindsay first attend Saturday afternoon tea with her and *the family*—Fancy Mae's mother, Summer Dae Perrier; Aunt Elizabeth Kate Lee, Summer Dae's sister who was named for Queen Elizabeth I; and Fancy Mae's sister, Jacqueline Anna Valentine. Although Lindsay had attended the teas, all the attention had been placed on her potential suitors. Within an hour, the family had decided whether or not the young men were worthy of second dates with Lindsay.

Needless to say, Lindsay didn't date very often.

The sun shined brightly on a clear, crisp Saturday as William drove his father's eight-year-old Buick to Lindsay's home. He felt calm until he parked the old car beside a new BMW in front of the Hiddleman mansion. Then the ole inferiority complex crept up again. William took a deep breath and told himself that he deserved to be there, even though his family didn't have as much money.

"Go, go, go," William whispered to motivate himself. He jumped out of the car and ran up the steps to the front door. He surveyed his attire to make sure he looked his best. No lint on the charcoal suit with navy pinstripes. No spots on the white shirt. No scuff marks on the polished black shoes. William was ready for an inspection by a military drill sergeant, but he still felt nervous as heck about meeting Lindsay's family.

Colonel Vanir's last orders ran through William's mind: "Be polite, son. Always say: yes, ma'am; yes, sir; please; and thank you. Smile and don't talk too much. Pull the chairs out for the ladies. Use just one lump of sugar. Take two lumps and you look like a sissy. Above all, double-knot your shoelaces."

William lifted his shaking hand to the door bell and pressed it just as the grandfather clock in the dining room chimed three times. At least he was punctual.

Fancy Mae, Elizabeth Kate, and Jacqueline Anna rushed to the door to greet William. Lindsay giggled. She felt surprised and delighted at how her mother and aunts fought to open the door for her date. Usually her mother asked the butler to escort the gentlemen into the house—alone.

Summer Dae, Lindsay's grandmother and the eldest member of the family, gracefully stepped down the staircase to join the others. She hurried for no one.

The four older women crowded around William like groupies at a rock concert. They smiled at him and put their hands on his broad shoulders. They took turns letting William escort them to an oblong table by a bay window in the formal living room. Each lady asked him questions about the incident.

"Has your arm healed, William?" Summer Dae inquired. As the matriarch, she always entered the dining room first. "Did the doctors give you a tetanus shot? You have no idea where that knife has been."

Elizabeth Kate said, "You must have been in great shape to fight those hideous gangsters. Do you work out?"

"Are those mean boys in jail?" Jacqueline Anna asked. She followed with the customary Southern phrase, "God bless their hearts."

"How on earth can we ever thank you enough for helping our darling Lindsay?" Fancy Mae asked. She turned and winked at Lindsay.

Lindsay continued to smile. She sensed this would be an easy afternoon for William, although she doubted she'd get in more than five words with her date.

Finally William escorted Lindsay to the table and helped her with her chair. She didn't ask any questions. She just told William that she was so proud of him. He blushed.

The butler seated William across the table from Lindsay, with the family between them. He had hoped to sit beside her. However, for today, simply being in the same room with Lindsay delighted him.

The ladies insisted that William tell the whole story of how he helped Lindsay and Mittens. William stumbled on his first words, and then he froze. Silence filled the formal living room, except for the tick-tock-tick-tock from the grandfather clock. Lindsay winked at William to help calm his nerves. He smiled and blushed. Now he had the courage to face any embarrassing moment, even stage fright at the Great Tea Initiation.

William told the whole story, from the first punch to Mittens and her kittens coming home. When he mentioned the kittens, Lindsay explained that she had asked William to name the yellow kitten that looked like a little tiger.

"Oh?" Summer Dae replied with raised eyebrows. "You mean the one we call Boxer?"

"Yes, ma'am," William replied. He sat up straight and announced, "That's short for Boxer Shorts."

Fancy Mae nearly dropped her Earl Grey tea in her lap. Elizabeth Kate giggled. Jacqueline Anna blushed and fanned her face with her hand. At that point, William realized he wasn't in the company of his college buddies. He hung his head and feared he'd never see Lindsay again.

Fortunately for William, the term *boxer shorts* triggered happy memories for Summer Dae. Her deceased husband had always worn them, refusing to even consider trying on "those tight things." After his death, Summer Dae gave away all his clothes except for three pairs of boxer shorts. She kept them in her top dresser drawer as a reminder of her true love.

Summer Dae cleared her throat and sternly stated, "I think that's a right fine name." Then she glared at the other ladies, one by one, until they got the message. "William, dear, I do hope you can escort our Lindsay to a matinee before you return to VMI. Perhaps y'all would enjoy dinner at Trudy's Restaurant. They do serve the finest shrimp grits and peach cobbler this side of Savannah."

With that, William had been declared an acceptable suitor for Lindsay. No other family member argued. They just politely drank their tea. Lindsay smiled at William and quietly clapped her hands under the table. All the women paused to look at William. They knew they'd see his face again and again.

Back at the Hospitality Station, William and his daughters clicked their tea cups together as a toast to a happy ending. Aria sat back in her chair and drank her last sip of tea. She felt proud of her father and wished she had just a smidgen of his tremendous courage.

"You are so brave, Dad! Spicy brave."

William smiled for a moment, and then his gaze drifted to the floor. Aria assumed his expressionless look meant he was remembering something he didn't want to discuss. She had learned not to pry when he was in one of those moods.

"If anything had happened to your mom," William muttered. He looked back at Aria and admitted, "I never would have forgiven myself."

Then William's eyes looked downward again, and he sighed. A painful memory churned in his mind, a moment of his deepest regret.

Chapter 4
The One Not Saved

In William's mind, he left the tea party with his daughters and journeyed back in time to the darkest moment of his life. He was about Aria's age, but larger and stronger than most boys in his class. He had made friends with a younger lad, Jeremy Hale, who lived with his mother three houses down the street. Now William wished he had never met the boy.

Although Jeremy was too ordinary and quiet to be popular, William enjoyed teaching him how to bat, catch, and pass a soccer ball. Jeremy was the little brother William never had. Mrs. Hale appreciated William's sports mentoring since Mr. Hale had died when Jeremy was only seven years old.

This particular fall Saturday afternoon, William was teaching Jeremy his favorite defensive moves for dodge ball. Jeremy had complained about always getting picked last for that sport in gym class, so William had promised to turn him into one of the sneakiest players ever. William remembered the warmth from the sun, Jeremy's goofy laugh when he finally learned to spin right and dunk, and that fateful moment when the ball bounced between two parked cars and into the street.

Jeremy chased after the ball, imagining that his classmates were cheering for him and his winning team. He never noticed the speeding car coming down the hill toward his wayward ball. The driver of the car, worried about being late for an appointment, didn't see the approaching ball.

William saw the speeding car and sprinted toward Jeremy, yelling for him to stop. Jeremy didn't hear him and kept chasing the ball.

William heard a hideous screeching sound as the driver slammed on his brakes to try to avoid hitting Jeremy, who was now in the middle of the road. William didn't care about his own safety as he leaped from the curb toward Jeremy.

The next two seconds went by in a blur. William pushed Jeremy out of the path of the car, and then he quickly rolled three times to avoid being hit as well. The car clipped William's right leg and then skidded to a stop several inches beyond where Jeremy had been running. Jeremy's mother and other neighbors ran out of their homes when they heard the commotion.

William slowly rose to his feet and hobbled to Jeremy's side. He hardly noticed his severe cuts, broken ankle, and dislocated shoulder because there was only one thing on his mind—the pool of blood near Jeremy's head. Jeremy had landed headfirst on the street.

After being in a coma for three weeks, Jeremy died.

William never forgave himself. He often ran different scenarios in his mind of how he could have saved Jeremy.

Perhaps he could have pulled Jeremy back instead of pushing him forward. Maybe he could have—somehow—signaled the driver to slow down and thus avoid the whole incident. Would he have had time to grab Jeremy, jump to the other side of the street, and land on his back to protect Jeremy from harm?

At Jeremy's funeral, William kept his head down and barely acknowledged anyone. Guilt overwhelmed him. He wished he had been the one to die, not Jeremy. William's father ordered him to tell Mrs. Hale that he was sorry for her loss—and not to cry. William shook his head and walked two steps toward their car.

"Brave times require brave men," Colonel Vanir explained as he grabbed William's uninjured shoulder. He pointed William in the direction of Mrs. Hale and gave him a push.

William waited for three other people to finish speaking with Mrs. Hale. Then he took a deep breath while lifting his head to face her.

"I'm sorry for your loss, Mrs. Hale. Jeremy is . . . was . . . a great friend. And Mrs. Hale," William turned so his father wouldn't catch sight of the tears in his eyes, "I'm so sorry I . . . I . . . I didn't save him. It's all my fault!"

"Nonsense, now," Mrs. Hale said as she continued to wipe the tears from her cheeks. "You did all you could, William. No need for apologies. The hours you spent with Jeremy were his happiest since his daddy died. He talked about you all the time. I know you meant no harm to come to him. It was an accident." Mrs. Hale lifted William's chin with her shaky hand. "But if it makes you feel any better, I forgive you." Mrs. Hale moved closer to William and kissed his forehead. "I forgive you."

William politely excused himself and walked away before Mrs. Hale could see the tears in his eyes. He wondered how any mother could possibly forgive him. William looked at the sky and prayed for God to take his wicked life, right then and there. The grief and shame were too great for him to endure one more second.

Please, God, I don't deserve to live. I don't deserve forgiveness. Let me die for what I've done. William closed his eyes and waited. Lightning didn't strike. A poisonous snake didn't bite him. A zombie didn't attack him.

After a few minutes of silence, William realized his prayer had gone unanswered. He felt angry and overwhelmed with guilt. William decided that if he wasn't going to die today, then he'd die another day protecting someone. He'd fight for country and family, like his father. But under no condition would he forgive himself for harming Jeremy.

Chapter 5
Leaving Vitchera

The first navigator of Mitushi's crew, PomPass, gently guided the fleet's finest superspaceship, *Rama XI*, out of the milky ocean and into the air a mile above the Gallion's city. Long ago the Gallions had built superspaceships that could maneuver through air, on land, and under water, which had given them trade and defense advantages over most other worlds. Hundreds of Gallions, who earlier had gathered on View Hill, now cheered and waved to their friends and family on the *Rama*. They all knew the importance—and dangers—of this first voyage to Earth.

PomPass slowly flew the *Rama* into orbit around Vitchera. When the ship was in position, he alerted Mitushi.

Mitushi had been monitoring the departure from the Central Viewing Chamber with other members of the royal family—Queen Supreme Nashata, Princess LeSom, and his wife, Orakakima.

Now that the *Rama* was in orbit, Mitushi and Orakakima marched down the main corridor to the Navigation Chamber. On either side of them, wide columns of white light spaced ten feet apart supported the ceilings. These columns, found everywhere in the superspaceship, were used instead of walls. Made of crystals and free energy, they also provided superior sources of light and communication for intergalactic travel.

Mitushi took his place at Central Control, which was a large circular platform in the middle of the Navigation Chamber. Central Control was protected with a cap of white light. Mitushi tapped this cover with one of his tentacles. It opened to expose an array of buttons, switches, bright lights, and star charts.

Orakakima stood on a platform below Mitushi. She joined tentacles with four other expert shielders, two on either side of her. The five of them used their thoughts and the free-energy columns in the *Rama* to form protective barriers wherever needed. Orakakima, the most renowned shielder on Vitchera, traveled with Mitushi on most of his missions. They formed an expert team to fly and protect superspaceships on even the most dangerous expeditions.

"Ready, Ora?" Mitushi asked. Orakakima's parents had called her Ora since birth. Except during ceremonies, everyone else used the nickname as well. Most importantly, Ora preferred it.

"Ready, Commander."

Mitushi touched a blue button in the right corner of Central Control and announced, "Attention all Gallions." His voice flowed from Central Control to the columns of white light so everyone would hear him. "This is the commander supreme. Brace yourself for wormhole entrance."

Mitushi glanced at the large viewing portal in front of the Navigation Chamber to see what was outside the *Rama*. A series of aqua and white circles, like a Slinky in space, appeared in front of them. This was the entrance to the Vitcheran Wormhole, a portal used for accelerated travel to the other side of the galaxy.

"Show exit of Vitcheran Wormhole," Mitushi ordered. PomPass pressed buttons on a smaller control panel in front of him. The other side of the wormhole appeared on the viewing portal.

Mitushi focused on the wormhole's exit, not the entrance. He spread the ends of his tentacles across Central Control so he could touch numerous buttons and switches simultaneously.

Central Control, as well as the columns of white lights, began to buzz and glow. The ship steadily flew to the front of the wormhole as Mitushi continued to focus on the wormhole's exit. In a few seconds, the ship was sucked into the wormhole and propelled to the other side of the galaxy.

Mitushi slowed the ship to a medium pace and ordered, "Standard view," so he could see their present position. PomPass modified the viewing portal. It showed the other side of the Vitcheran Wormhole, just a few clicks from where Mitushi had focused.

Mitushi made a ship-wide announcement, "Attention all Gallions. We've traversed the wormhole. Commence standard duties."

The crew cheered. Ora and her assistant shielders relaxed their minds and tentacles. Although Mitushi had made the wormhole passage look easy, it was the most complicated maneuver known to Gallion spaceship captains.

Mitushi used the star charts on Central Control to plot a course to the next wormhole, which he transmitted to PomPass. Then he and Ora returned to the Central Viewing Chamber.

As soon as they entered the chamber, the queen demanded, "When will we arrive on Earth?"

"We must travel through two more wormholes to reach the center of the Milky Way Galaxy," Mitushi calmly explained. He was quite used to his mother's impatience. "Then it's a short jump to Earth. About two Earth weeks will pass until we arrive."

"Splendid," the queen replied. "Now we must review our plans for peaceful contact with the humans. Before we departed I observed the youngirl, Aria Vanir, from the Gallery of Worlds. I'm quite excited about meeting her. She possesses very strong gifts of future visions and remote sightings, which unfortunately she hides because humans . . . well . . . just don't get it. This explains why she was able to view our land from so very far away. I believe her skills will grow stronger during her Earth teen years. We must make a good impression on her so she doesn't shut down entirely and become another boring geek."

"Or worse," Mitushi warned, "destructive aliens like the Macidopians might get to her first and ruin her divine path."

Princess LeSom gasped at the thought of a Macidopian even touching youngirl Aria Vanir, especially after what they had done to Miley Cyrus.

"Ora," the queen continued, "have you and the other shielders prepared camouflage for our journey from the third wormhole to Earth? I don't want any government satellites or telescopes to detect us."

Ora bowed her head and replied, "Done, Your Majesty."

"Splendid! Now I want you to serve as our official ambassador supreme on this vital diplomatic mission. From what I've observed of the youngirl, she's quite attached to her mother. I'm concerned that my available ambassadors, although quite seasoned in intergalactic protocol, would come across as grumpy old men to her. You enjoy protecting and nurturing. I believe the two of you will enjoy spending time together and learning about each other's culture."

Ora felt honored by this vital assignment. She bowed to the queen as a gesture of utmost respect.

Princess LeSom stretched one of her tentacles seven feet and tapped her older sister on the back.

"Yes?" Queen Supreme Nashata asked with hesitation in her voice.

Princess LeSom cleared her throat and announced, "I would like to give a concert . . ."

"No!" the queen abruptly interrupted. "That noise makes my whiskers tremble."

"Nashata, let me finish," Princess LeSom pleaded. "A concert of famous Earth music. I downloaded more than one million tunes from the Gallery of Worlds into my vocal whiskers."

The queen paused to consider her sister's request. It seemed innocent and sincere, but the queen had discovered how easily LeSom could really screw up even the simplest diplomatic assignment. However, Queen Supreme Nashata also had observed the importance that humans placed on their music.

"Very well, you can perform a short concert as I entertain Aria with a royal tea party." Princess LeSom's whiskers spiked, and she clapped her tentacles together. "But I," the queen added in a stern voice, "pick out the music." LeSom's whiskers wilted to the side of her face.

"A tea party?" Ora said with a questioning tone.

"One of their friendship rituals I've observed," the queen replied. "Either that or a slumber party, and I don't believe they make sleeping bags in our sizes. I've made my decision.

We'll have a grand tea for Aria to meet me. We'll do it Gallion style, if you know what I mean. Ora, would you please work with my handmaidens to make arrangements? I want this to be a perfect event."

Ora bowed her head to the queen and replied, "My pleasure, Your Majesty."

"Thank you. Now Mitushi, has your engineering department configured a communication device that I can use to access Aria's tDiary?"

"It's being tested as we speak, Mother. We had challenges modifying our signals to match such primitive technology. It should be ready by the time we reach the second wormhole."

"Splendid. The youngirl quite enjoys writing in this toy. She uses it to express her thoughts and feelings, tell about her day, and explain her predictions. In a way, this tDiary serves as a good friend to her. Let's hope she continues to treat it as a friend by the time we finish with it."

Chapter 6
Protecting Aria

On Friday, June 2, near the Virginia Beach Middle School softball field, Aria played catch with her close friends Meredith Spheeris and Tommy Manger. The physical education teacher called them to join their classmates at home plate for a game. Aria wanted to fix her lopsided ponytail, so Meredith and Tommy ran ahead. Eric Watts, the largest and meanest kid in seventh grade, saw Aria by herself. He knew this was his time for revenge.

Aria had never done anything to hurt Eric—not intentionally anyway. Their teacher had made him sit beside her so she'd be a good influence on him, academically and socially. Eric had repeated first and second grades. He was just as slow with making friends as he was with numbers. Eric felt angry at Aria because she didn't help him cheat on tests, hadn't written a paper for him, and refused to lie for him. Eric thought Aria was wicked.

As Aria struggled to smooth her tangled hair, Eric and his only two friends crowded around her. Eric's friends were almost as tall as he was and tried to be just as tough.

"Where you goin', prissy girl?" Eric asked as he got in Aria's face.

"Prissy girl, prissy girl," the other two boys chanted. They wanted to be just like their hero, Eric.

Aria lifted her trembling hand and pointed to their classmates on the softball field. Eric slapped her hand with a hard whack. The three bullies laughed at Aria, who was on the verge of crying.

Eric grabbed Aria's shoulders and said, "Looks like you're late, prissy girl." Then he lifted her until they were eye-to-eye, shook her, and tossed her to the ground. Aria's head hit a large tree branch that had fallen last weekend during a thunder storm.

"Don't tell anyone about this, prissy girl. Unless you want a few broken ribs the next time." Eric started to leave with his friends, but then he turned and quipped, "If you weren't so clumsy, you wouldn't fall down so much."

The impact left her with cuts under her left eye and a banging headache. Worst of all, she felt too scared to tell anyone the truth. When Aria's teacher noticed the cuts, Aria lied that she had tripped over the branch while running.

Aria's teacher immediately called Lindsay when she learned about the accident. Lindsay took Aria to the hospital on Naval Air Station Oceana, where William was stationed. Doctors ran tests on Aria's head. Aside from the cuts and a large bruise on her temple, she was fine.

That night, after their parents had gone to bed, Jackie sneaked into Aria's bedroom. She put her hand over her Aria's mouth and shined a flashlight in her eyes.

"Peanut," Jackie whispered. She had given Aria that nickname several years ago because of Aria's small size. Since her parents had expressed their displeasure with the nickname, Jackie used it only when she was alone with Aria. "Don't yell or say anything. You don't want to get in trouble, do you?"

Aria shook her head. After her tough day at school, she didn't want to fight about anything. Jackie removed her hand from Aria's mouth.

In a soft voice, Aria whispered, "Get that light out of my eyes."

Jackie kept the light in Aria's face and replied, "After you tell me what really happened on the playground."

"What do you mean?" Aria asked. She grabbed the covers and pulled them to her chin. "I told you. I fell on the tree branch while I was running."

"Nuke that lie!" Jackie said sternly, but not loudly enough to wake their parents. "I've seen you jump and spin in ballet recitals. And you've done that yoga tree pose thing for three solid minutes. Don't tell me you tripped and fell." Aria just shrugged her shoulders. She still felt too scared about getting beat up again. Jackie lowered her voice and said, "Okay, Tommy told me he saw Eric Watts pick you up and throw you on top of that branch like it was a professional wrestlin' match."

The pressure to tell the truth proved to be too much for Aria. She pulled the covers over her head and started to cry. Jackie turned off the flashlight and sat beside her sister. She started to pat Aria on the shoulder but stopped because she didn't want to appear soft.

"Get me a Kleenex," Aria mumbled. Jackie grabbed a box of tissues from Aria's nightstand while Aria sat up in bed to face her. "Why would Tommy snitch on me?"

"He told only me, and I made him promise not to tell anyone else. Your secret is safe with us. We figured that, with school ending next week and teachers being in a lax mood, Eric would only get a slap on the wrist. But I'm on a mission of revenge. With me, it's personal."

Jackie smiled. The left side of her mouth curled up higher. Aria had noticed this can't-wait-to-fight grin on Jackie's face before a karate competition or soccer game. Aria giggled and hugged her big sister.

Jackie chuckled and then said, "Don't get all emotional on me now." Jackie halfheartedly patted Aria's back and then gently pushed her away. "We have a lot of work to do," Jackie continued. "We have to gather intel, run simulations, and prepare for our attack. Got it?" Aria rubbed her hand under her nose and nodded.

"Use a tissue, Peanut."

The next morning, Aria told Jackie everything she knew about Eric. What he looked like. How he walked and talked. Where he hung out before school, after classes, and during recess. When his bus arrived and departed. They thought of three plans to lure Eric to Jackie and practiced them in their yard that afternoon. By supper, they had agreed on their best game plan.

On Sunday, they ran simulations in the yard three more times and discussed contingency strategies if anything went wrong. Jackie spent two extra hours on intense karate training. Even though Eric was still in the seventh grade, he was her age and two sizes larger. She prepared for a tough match against him and, if needed, his two buddies.

Monday afternoon, when the bell rang to end the last class of high school, Jackie sprinted across the street to Virginia Beach Middle School. She hid behind a green dumpster, where she changed into black sweats and a ski mask she had stuffed into her book bag.

Outside the middle school, Aria nervously tossed a piece of gravel at Eric. Missed. She picked up a larger stone, aimed more carefully, and this time hit him on the back. As planned, Eric started to chase Aria. She ran with all her might to the dumpster where Jackie was hiding.

On the way, Eric yelled at his two bully friends. They ran after him.

Aria ran past the dumpster and climbed a nearby tree where she could keep an eye on Jackie. When Eric reached the dumpster, Jackie sprang out in front of him. She nailed a sliding side kick to his chest and quickly followed with a spinning swing kick to the side of his head.

Eric stumbled backward, but he didn't fall. He tried to punch Jackie in the face, but she dodged his fist with ease.

Jackie noticed two boys who matched the description of Eric's goons running toward her. She knew she had to act fast. She hit Eric's head with a back fist and socked a middle punch to his stomach. Eric moaned and fell to the ground.

Jackie twirled three times to create distance between her and the two approaching boys. She picked up a long stick and practiced the most difficult combinations of her kata.

The two boys stopped suddenly. They looked at Jackie first, then Eric, and finally each other. Immediately they turned around and ran back to school.

Jackie rolled Eric onto his stomach and pulled his arms behind his back. She pressed her knee against his wrists to keep him on the ground.

Jackie lowered her voice and concentrated on mimicking a New York mobster, "You or your gang so much as look at Aria and you're goin' to the docks next time. I'm talkin' cement blocks. Got it?" Eric didn't move, even if he could. With her free hand, Jackie grabbed his hair and moved his head up and down to make it look like he was nodding. "Good. You tell anyone this happened, and I break a few ribs next time. Maybe even four. Got it?" Jackie again pulled Eric's hair so his head nodded. In her normal voice, Jackie concluded, "Besides, you don't want anyone to know that a girl beat your ass. Ha-ha-ha-ha-ha!"

Aria climbed down the tree and tied a handkerchief around her face as a disguise. She ran to where Jackie had pinned Eric. Aria untied Eric's shoes and took off his dirty socks. Jackie bound Eric's hands with the laces while Aria poked one of his stinky socks in his mouth.

With their mission accomplished, the Vanir girls tossed their disguises in the dumpster and sprinted to catch their bus. They promised each other that this incident would be their secret for the rest of their lives.

That night, after everyone in the Vanir family had gone to bed, Aria sneaked into Jackie's bedroom. She put her hand over Jackie's mouth and shined a flashlight in her eyes.

Jackie pushed Aria's hand away and quickly grabbed the flashlight from her.

"What do you think you're doing, Peanut?"

Aria giggled and hugged her big sister. This time, Jackie hugged her back. Tightly.

"Thank you so much for what you did today," Aria whispered into her sister's ear. "You protected me, just like Dad did for Mom and Mittens. That must mean you really, really love me. And not just because I'm your sister. Don't you?"

Jackie didn't reply. Like her father, she wasn't comfortable expressing emotions. Aria grabbed a fistful of Jackie's hair and gently moved her head up and down. The girls laughed and released their hug.

Jackie smiled at Aria and softly said, "Of course I love you, Peanut. I'll always protect you. Promise. We Vanir girls have to stick together."

Chapter 7
The Queen's First Message

Queen Supreme Nashata swiftly moved from her royal suite on the *Rama* to Holospace Five. She anxiously tapped a tentacle tip on the shield of the holospace to unlock it. Mitushi, Ora, and First Engineer Peakte were already inside and greeted the queen. Mitushi had requested his mother's presence because the holospace was ready for her first contact with Aria Vanir.

Holospaces were rooms filled with a matrix of small white columns. These columns, like the larger ones supporting the ship, were composed of free energy and crystals. They stored and displayed data in six dimensions so Gallions could experience personal interactions with beings on distant worlds. This particular holospace had been programmed with information about Earth, specifically the life of Aria Vanir.

Peakte explained how a short, white column in the center of Holospace Five had been designed to connect with Aria's tDiary. He nicknamed it Tay Com, short for tDiary Communicator. He showed the queen how she could speak into the Tay Com and her words would appear as a journal entry in Aria's tDiary. Peakte then described an upgrade to the Tay Com that would allow the queen to dialogue with Aria as though they were speaking face to face.

The queen's whiskers parted into a U as she exclaimed, "Splendid, Peakte. Impressive work. Now, how soon can I talk to Aria? We have much to discuss."

Ora warned, "Remember, Your Majesty, humans generally fear anything new. May I suggest you send a short, pleasant message to Aria's tDiary as a start? Then you can work up to a holospace dialogue."

The queen reluctantly agreed. Mitushi asked Peakte to prepare the Tay Com for her first communication with Aria. When it was ready, the queen spoke.

> *Calling Aria Vanir. I am Queen Supreme Nashata, Galactic Mother of the Gallions. We live on the planet Vitchera in the Jenegu Galaxy. We are the ones who live in small mountains with no trees by a milky ocean in which birds and fish swim. Yes, you saw our world quite accurately.*
>
> *The Gallions accept your invitation to Virginia Beach and bring you blessings of great peace. Our mission is to establish a harmonious relationship with you so we learn more about each other and our cultures. To you I extend an invitation for a dialogue. If you wish to accept, please write to me in your tDiary.*
>
> *I look forward to a long and cherished friendship.*
>
> *Queen Supreme Nashata.*

The queen stepped back from the Tay Com and asked, "Will I hear back from Aria?"

"Indeed, indeed," Peakte answered.

"Well, how soon?"

Peakte explained, "She must open her tDiary and turn it on for the message to appear. Then it is just a matter of the youngirl answering you."

"Where is she now?" the queen demanded.

Peakte nervously replied, "The Tay Com can display images of the youngirl's environment. Let me show you." Peakte tapped two tentacle tips on the top of the Tay Com. A multidimensional picture of Aria's backyard appeared in the air above the Tay Com. The Gallions watched Aria as she sat in a swing on the covered porch and read *Galactic Gina*.

"Can we float the tDiary from her bedroom to the porch swing so she'll open it?" the queen asked.

Mitushi replied, "Mother, do you want to give the youngirl the fright of her life?"

Ora responded, "Remember, they are primitive humans. They've learned to resort to fear when they experience something . . . out of their world."

The whiskers on the queen's head moved side-to-side as she pondered how to urge Aria to open her tDiary. She knew she needed to meet Aria on the youngirl's level.

A few minutes later the queen's whiskers spiked as she exclaimed, "I have a plan. A brilliant plan."

"What, Mother?"

"The youngirl has the gift of intuition and remote sightings. Let's see how good she really is." Queen Supreme Nashata touched the tips of her tentacles to her heart. Her whiskers swayed as she focused on the center of Aria's forehead. The Queen sent mental images to Aria of the *Rama*, tDiary, and Gallion land.

On Earth, Aria felt queasy, like she was about to receive a prediction. She saw an image of a large, oval object in space.

The top two-thirds was blue-gray, the rest yellowish white. It reminded Aria of pictures she had seen in science class of blue whales, except without the fins and tail. Aria decided to look more closely inside this flying whale. She saw rows of tall, white lights in hallways and golden creatures that looked like walking jellyfish.

Then Aria saw a picture of her tDiary in front of her. She thought it meant someone was trying to access her tDiary and read her secrets. Aria panicked. She dropped her book on the porch swing, ran up to her room, and opened the top of her tDiary.

The message from the queen automatically uploaded. Aria clumsily plopped into the chair at her desk. She was far more focused on the tDiary screen than where she was trying to sit. Aria slowly read the queen's statement. Again. And again.

"Astro," Aria whispered. She thought to herself, *somebody—or something—really is out there.*

Aria pressed her thumb against the tScan to save the queen's entry. Then she wrote her reply.

> *Thursday, June 15, 2028*
> *Hi Queen Supreme Nashata. I've never talked to a queen before, but you sound really nice. I accept your invitation for a dialogue. You can be my new best friend for the day. Tommy is my regular best friend, but he's not a queen.*
> *Your friend,*
> *Aria.*
> *P.S. By the way, are you inside the starship that looks like a flying blue whale?*

Chapter 8
The Dialogue

In Holospace Five, Queen Supreme Nashata and the other Gallions cheered with great delight when they received Aria's message. They felt tremendous joy and relief with the success of having made a positive first contact with the youngirl. The queen even wrapped her tentacles around everyone. This was the Gallion way of hugging.

The queen looked at Ora and asked, "Wouldn't you now agree that the youngirl is ready for dialogue?" Ora nodded. "Splendid! Let's commence."

"Your Majesty, stand in front of the Tay Comm," Peakte instructed. "Now touch both sides of it and hold tight."

"Like this?" the queen asked.

"Indeed, indeed!" Peakte felt immensely proud to have the queen using one of his prized inventions.

On Earth, Aria leaned back in her chair and waited for words to appear on the screen of her tDiary. Nothing happened. She clicked the *Save* button three times to ensure her message to the queen had been sent. Finally, an image of Queen Supreme Nashata projected from the screen into the air above the tDiary.

Seeing the tall, golden creature with tentacles and whiskers shocked Aria. She screamed and fell back in her chair. Lindsay ran down the hallway to Aria's bedroom. Aria quickly closed the cover of her tDiary so her mother wouldn't see the *thing* coming out of it. When Lindsay asked what was wrong, Aria said she was practicing a new ballet move and had accidentally fallen against her chair. Lindsay looked at Aria's legs to make sure she was okay, and then she left the bedroom.

"Told you they react with fear," Ora reminded the queen, whose whiskers had wilted to the side of her face. "She'll get over it though, so don't take it personally. Remember *E.T.*?"

Aria cautiously returned to her desk. She stared at the tDiary for a few minutes, debating what to do. Open it. Toss it. Nuke it. Tell Dad. Forget everything.

The queen decided to send Aria a mental image of herself with two tentacle tips in the air to make the peace sign. She had learned about this gesture while watching tapes of the Earth's 1960s in the Gallery of Worlds. Hopefully this would encourage Aria to move past her fears and start a dialogue.

It worked. Aria carefully opened her tDiary and again saw the image of Queen Supreme Nashata. This time, Aria just took a deep breath and stared at the freakish alien. On the *Rama*, a picture of Aria at her desk with her tDiary emerged above the Tay Com.

"You can talk to the youngirl now," Peakte whispered to the queen.

Ora quickly muttered, "Keep it simple."

The queen nodded her head and said, "Greetings, Aria Vanir. I am Nashata, Queen Supreme of the Gallions on Vitchera." Aria bowed her head in respect. "We received the call you sent to all aliens from your tDiary. Quite impressive, I must admit."

Aria felt stunned, yet curious. She poked her finger at the image of the queen just for fun. Her finger went right through the projection.

"We have a device," the queen explained, "that shows us images of each other. I see you at your desk, and you see me aboard our superspaceship." Aria sat up straight in her chair and smoothed her hair, which had gotten messed up when she tumbled over her chair.

Aria's voice trembled as she mumbled, "Can . . . can you hear me?"

"Quite well."

Aria cleared her throat and clearly stated, "Welcome to Earth. I'm Aria. Guess you knew that. I don't have a title, but I'll be in eighth grade next year." By now, Aria felt more comfortable talking to this alien leader, and she wanted to ask some questions. "By the way, is your spaceship that blue-whale thing in the sky?"

The queen's whiskers curled as she tried to recall learning about blue whales in the Gallery of Worlds. She drew a blank.

"Manifester, show me a blue whale from Earth," the queen ordered.

In the front-right corner of the holospace, the manifester—a unique combination of crystals—began to glow and buzz. The Gallions used manifesters to view and create things.

A feminine voice from the manifest machine said, "A blue whale from Earth, Your Majesty." A picture of a blue whale appeared at the front of the holospace. The Gallions made ooh and aah sounds. "Do you wish to manifest at this time, or continue viewing?"

"View only," the queen quickly responded. "Do you know how hard it would be to get a whale through customs?" The queen walked around the image of the blue whale to inspect its entire body. "If you remove the fins, tail, and crusty things from that creature, it does bear some resemblance to our superspaceship."

"What's a superspaceship?" Aria asked.

"The largest version of space-travel vessels in our fleet."

"How fast does it go?"

"Faster than the speed of light, especially through wormholes."

"Astro!" Aria exclaimed. "I didn't know anything could travel faster than the speed of light."

"Quite so, youngirl. It's the speed of infinity. Altability, actually. Our pilots simply focus on being all together in two places at once. Where they are, and where they want to be. Then they and their ships automatically move from where they are to their destinations. This requires considerable focus and practice. Humans have the potential for altability, but they are too bound by time and space to put it into practice. At least, for now."

"How far away is your planet—Victor something?"

"Vitchera is three galaxies from Earth."

"Astro!"

The queen turned to Mitushi and whispered, "Tell LeSom to come here immediately. I can't understand why this girl keeps referring to a baseball team. Must be a special dialect or code. I need an interpreter." Mitushi touched a light-blue crystal on his right tentacle to contact Princess LeSom.

"Where are y'all now?" Aria asked.

The queen turned to Ora and softly mumbled, "Quite inquisitive, isn't she?" Then she replied to Aria, "On the opposite end of your Milky Way Galaxy."

"Aria!" Lindsay called. "Time for lunch. Sandwiches and chocolate pudding."

Aria quickly said, "I have to go soon. Are y'all coming to Virginia Beach? Do you want to stay with us? Where are you landing the blue-whale ship? How many people—I mean Gallions—are coming? Maybe y'all should wear robes and hats. Everyone will go nuclear when they see you."

Queen Supreme Nashata turned to Princess LeSom, who had entered Holospace Five when Aria's mother was calling her. The whiskers on the queen's head were curled because she didn't understand Aria's last two sentences.

LeSom understood the confusion and translated, "Everyone will get scared when they see us because we look alien to them."

The queen responded to Aria, "I've established peaceful, diplomatic relations on several worlds where natives went nuclear when they first met us. Leave it to me. I have a plan."

LeSom nudged her sister and added, "*Y'all* is a Southern term for singular you or plural you. Known in other parts of the country as *yuns*, *you guys*, or *dudes*."

The queen boasted, "I actually knew that from watching NASCAR in the Gallery of Worlds, I'll have you know."

"Aria, honey, we're waiting on you," Lindsay yelled down the hall.

"My mom is—"

The queen interrupted, "Open your tDiary tonight, when you can talk again. And Aria, tell no one of our dialogue. No one, not even your mother. As you said, they will . . . go nuclear."

Chapter 9
The Queen's Invitation

That night, while the rest of her family watched a movie on tHTV, Aria opened her tDiary to continue her discussion with the alien queen. She had kept her promise not to tell anyone about the Gallions, although she had asked her mother when Grandma Fancy Mae had planned to make her annual visit. That wasn't until mid-July, so Aria had assumed the Gallions could stay until then. When Aria turned on her tDiary, the Tay Com sent signals to the royal family and Peakte. They all rushed to Holospace Five.

Queen Supreme Nashata touched the sides of the Tay Com with her tentacles and said, "Greetings, Aria."

Aria cheerfully replied, "Hello." She again poked her finger through the image of the queen. The queen's golden skin reflected like a ray of sunshine on Aria's flesh. Aria whispered to herself, "Must be real."

"Oh, we are quite real," the queen said. Her tone sounded more relaxed and calm now. The anxiety of first contact had ended. "Just as real as your family."

Aria looked surprised and asked, "You know about Mom, Dad, and Jackie?"

"We have studied civilizations on Earth for thousands of years. Most recently we've taken quite an interest in your space travel to your moon and Mars. We also monitor the satellites in your orbit. Most of all, we watch CNN."

"Astro!"

Queen Supreme Nashata, with curled whiskers, turned to Princess LeSom for slang interpretation.

"Great," LeSom said. "Wow. Fantastic. Awesome. Wonderful."

The queen turned to Aria and replied, "Yes . . . astro. Now, we must discuss plans for our visit."

"You can come any time before July thirteenth. We have spicy splash fireworks on the Fourth of July."

"*Splash* means trendy, stylish, popular, edgy," LeSom added to help the queen. "*Spicy splash*, top-of-the-charts best."

"Your kind invitation to join you in Virginia Beach delights us so," the queen stated in her most diplomatic tone. She knew the Gallions couldn't appear on Earth—it would cause mass panic. Ora had encouraged the queen to decline Aria's invitation gently because youngirls often took rejection so personally. "We graciously appreciate your thoughtfulness and courage. I would propose an alternative, Aria, which I believe you will find quite . . . astro."

Aria sat up straight in her chair and said, "Oh? What's that?"

"Come aboard our superspaceship, the *Rama XI*. We've modified certain chambers, called holospaces, to mimic the healthiest and most beautiful places on Earth. You will be quite safe here, I promise."

"Me, on the big blue whale in the sky?"

"If you wish to accept my most humble invitation," the queen responded. "The Gallion nation would be quite honored to have you as our guest aboard the *Rama*."

"Whoa," Aria whispered. "Imagine me, aboard a superspaceship, flying in the sky." Then Aria yelled, "Funtastic!"

The queen felt confused by Aria's reply. She turned to LeSom for a translation.

"That means yes," Princess LeSom explained. "From her expression, I can tell she's really excited."

"Splendid!" the queen exclaimed. "Three days from now, we will transmit an entry to your tDiary with information about your . . . boarding procedures. Look for a blinking green light on your tDiary. This is your signal that we've sent you the message."

"So you're beaming me aboard?" Aria asked.

"Something like that. Mitushi, my son and the commander supreme of our Gallion Fleet, will give you more details in the transmission. It will all be in your tDiary."

"Astro. What do I need to bring? Should I pack like I'm going to camp?"

"Bring whatever you want. We can materialize anything else you need in the holospace."

Aria leaned back in her chair. She felt overwhelmed and a bit dizzy just thinking about the outer space trip.

"Remember, Aria," Queen Supreme Nashata said in a low, stern voice. "Tell no one."

Chapter 10
Aria's Secret

On June 17, a Saturday, the Vanir and Manger families played at the beach. Tommy Manger poured saltwater from his pail into the moat of the sandcastle he had built with Aria. After Tommy's mother, Elizabeth, put more sunscreen on his fair shoulders and freckled cheeks, Tommy ran back to the ocean to get more water. While he was away, Aria used her finger to sketch the Gallion superspaceship in the sand beside the castle. Only two days had passed since the queen had asked Aria to keep their talks a secret. Aria had kept her promise. So far.

When Tommy arrived with the second pail of water, he wanted to know if the oval represented a nearby village or an enemy camp. Aria quickly brushed away the drawing and mumbled that it was nothing. The spaceship image reminded Aria of the day she had met Tommy three years ago at the Shake Place.

William Vanir had just moved his family to Virginia Beach, where he would be stationed with SEAL Team Three. Jackie and Aria knew no one. Tommy Manger's mother was a lieutenant serving on William's team as the communications specialist. Since their kids were about the same age, Elizabeth had suggested that the two families grab milkshakes and hang out at the beach. She had been an army brat and knew how difficult it was to make friends in a new place.

Tommy and Aria had sat together in the Shake Place, but they hadn't said a word to each other. Tommy had liked dinosaurs and trucks more than girls, and Aria had assumed Tommy knew nothing about ballet.

Bored, Tommy had started drawing a space battleship on his napkin. Aria had recognized the sketch from a funny sci-fi movie she had watched before moving to Virginia Beach. They ended up talking nonstop about the battleship, characters, and aliens in the movie. Aria and Tommy had found their common passions: science fiction and spaceships. Since then they had been best buddies.

"For the third time, Aria, go get some sand for the watchtower," Tommy pleaded. Aria shook her head, and the daydream left her mind.

"I'm not into sandcastles today," Aria calmly explained. She asked her mother if she could walk from the naval beach to the pier. Elizabeth Manger asked Tommy to go with her. Although Aria really wanted space, she reluctantly agreed to Tommy's company.

"Hey, are you extramad at me?" Tommy asked when they were away from their families.

Aria shook her head and mumbled, "No, just thinkin'."

"'bout what?"

"Nothin'," Aria replied. She stopped walking and said, "Tommy, do you believe in aliens? For real. Not just in books or movies. Real, live, aliens."

Tommy looked up in the sunny sky. He didn't see any stars, but he imagined them.

"Sure, I guess so."

Aria whispered, "Have you seen any real, live aliens?"

Tommy widened his eyes and said, "No-oooo." Then he made a freaky face and weird noises to sound like a creature from outer space.

Aria felt upset by Tommy's teasing. She frowned and quickly walked away.

Tommy caught up with Aria and pleaded, "Ah, don't go all nuclear on me. I was just joking. Lighten up!"

Aria blurted, "Well if you had seen the aliens I've seen, you wouldn't make jokes." Aria slapped her hand over her mouth and wished she could take back the last 30 seconds.

Tommy rarely heard Aria joke about anything, and she was a terrible liar. He and Jackie had never been able to ask Aria to make up false excuses to get them out of trouble with their parents. And so, when Aria mentioned seeing aliens, Tommy knew something astro had happened.

"Have you seen aliens?" Tommy whispered. He motioned for Aria to sit down in a secluded area of the beach where no one would hear them.

"I can't tell you. I promised."

For the next fifteen minutes, Tommy drilled Aria about the aliens. She continued to explain that she had made a promise not to tell anyone. The more Aria clammed up, the more Tommy persisted. Finally, he gave up.

"Fine then!" Tommy yelled. He jumped to his feet and picked up a handful of sand. "Don't tell me. I bet the whole thing never really happened. You've been reading too many sci-fi books. It's messing with your head. You always were weird!" Tommy threw the sand aside and stormed away.

That evening, Aria sat on the edge of her bed and gazed at her tDiary. Doubts ran through her mind.

Did I really see the Gallion queen? Is the queen's first message really saved in my tDiary? Are the Gallions really going to beam me aboard the Rama? *Am I going crazy? Maybe I am weird.* Aria slowly walked to her tDiary. *What if these Gallions are bad aliens who want to kidnap me? What if they want to experiment on me? What if Jackie and her friends are pulling a prank on me?*

Aria touched the top of her tDiary. For the first time in her life, she felt uncomfortable being near it. Almost, scared.

That's it, Aria convinced herself. *I need to tell Tommy. If he says the aliens are astro real, then I'll let them beam me on their ship. If not, I'll nuke the whole trip. I won't even talk to the octopus-arms queen anymore.*

Aria called Tommy and asked him to visit her. He refused at first, but she promised to tell him about the spaceship. With his parents' permission, Tommy rode his scootercycle three blocks to Aria's house.

First things first, Aria made Tommy promise to never ever tell anyone what she was about to show him. He quickly agreed. He felt anxious to learn Aria's big secret. Aria nervously showed Tommy her tDiary entry of May 22ⁿᵈ in which she invited an alien family to visit her at the beach.

Tommy shrugged his shoulders and asked, "What's the big deal about that?"

Aria whispered, "Someone answered." Tommy rolled his eyes to the ceiling and folded his arms across his chest. Aria just shook her head and scrolled to the queen's reply. "Look," Aria demanded as she pointed to her tDiary screen. "The Gallions are coming."

Tommy read the queen's reply to Aria. It sounded like a grown-up, not something Aria would write. If he had read this message in anyone else's journal, he'd assume it was a joke. He knew Aria was too serious and honest to lie about visiting aliens. Tommy leaned closer to the tDiary and reread the page. He started to believe.

"They're supposed to send me another message tomorrow," Aria explained.

"Huh?" Tommy mumbled. He still felt stunned.

"Tomorrow they'll tell me when and where I'm supposed to go to meet them." Aria felt excited and relieved to tell this to her friend. She assumed his silence meant he believed her, so she kept talking. "Tommy, I think they're going to beam me aboard their superspaceship. That's the oval thing I was drawing in the sand today."

Lindsay knocked on Aria's bedroom door and said, "Tommy?" Aria rushed to close the lid on her tDiary before her mother opened the door. "Your mom called, and she wants you to go home now. It's almost dark."

Tommy strained to reply, "Yeah . . . ah . . . okay."

Lindsay looked puzzled as she asked, "Tommy, are you okay? You look like you've seen a ghost."

"I . . . ah . . . guess I'm just hungry?"

"I'll fix you a couple of peanut butter crackers. Stop by the kitchen before you leave." Lindsay left Aria's bedroom and walked into the kitchen.

"Do you believe me?" Aria asked Tommy in a soft voice.

Tommy sat in Aria's chair and whispered, "Real live aliens contacted you. Astro!"

Unclear about his response, Aria sternly repeated, "Do you believe me?"

"Now I do" Tommy admitted. "You get to be a real Galactic Gina!" Tommy balled his fist and tapped Aria on the shoulder to congratulate her. She chuckled and blushed. Tommy started to leave, but Aria grabbed him by the arm.

"Remember," Aria warned, "tell no one."

Chapter 11
Drake's Opinion

As soon as Tommy arrived home that night, he ran through the house to find his seventeen-year-old brother, Drake. Shouts and fake gunfire upstairs compelled Tommy to burst into Drake's bedroom without knocking. As Tommy had suspected, Drake and his friends were playing war games on tVid. An advanced holographic video game displayed images of the enemies into the center of Drake's bedroom. Drake and his buddies were trying to escape from prison without being detected. Tommy's pesky interruption ruined their plans, and everyone got captured again. The teen boys felt extramad at Tommy and tried to kick him out of Drake's room. Tommy resisted. He had always wanted to play tVid, but Drake had told him he was too clumsy and slow. Really, Tommy just wanted to be like Drake. In an effort to stay in the room and possibly play tVid, Tommy said he knew a secret about aliens.

Drake tugged at Tommy's shirt and said, "Out with it, dude, or we feed you to the prison rats."

Tommy knew he wasn't supposed to tell anyone about the Gallions, but he felt excited by all the attention. He believed that sharing knowledge of the aliens would give him a golden pass to play games with Drake and the older guys. Tommy longed to be accepted by them.

"Aria Vanir. She's . . . she's . . ." Tommy's voice started to quiver. In fact, his whole body trembled.

"What?" Drake demanded. "Is Aria an alien?"

All the boys laughed at Tommy. He felt ashamed.

"No, dude. The aliens are coming here. They want Aria to visit their superspaceship. She's going to meet their queen."

Drake and his friends roared with laughter. To them, fighting with fake images was more real than little Tommy's lie about Aria visiting aliens.

"Stupid kid," Drake teased. "Did Aria and Jackie put you up to this?"

Drake's friends followed his lead, mocking Tommy and laughing at him.

"Sucker! Ha, ha, ha."

"Loser!"

"Will Tom-Tom save the little girl from the mean aliens? Ha, ha, ha."

"Everybody knows aliens don't exist. Liar!"

Tommy ran out of Drake's room and into his bedroom. He felt so miserable and sad. He'd never get to play tVid now, much less face Drake's friends again. He figured he might as well die now.

Tommy wanted to cry, but he knew that was for sissies. He needed an outlet for all his anger and humiliation. Believing in Aria had caused him tremendous ridicule from his older brothers. She must pay! Tommy decided to call Aria and let her have it.

When Tommy called, Aria inserted her earpiece and pulled up his image on her tBinder. Now they could talk face to face.

"Hi, Tommy," Aria said when she had completed the connection. She noticed Tommy's flushed face. "You look extramad. What are you nuked about?"

Tommy lashed out, "You! You're a loser. Everybody knows aliens don't exist. Liar!"

Aria felt baffled. Less than an hour ago, Tommy had said he believed her. Now he was calling her a liar.

"It's true, Tommy. You saw the message from the Gallion queen."

"You and Jackie put me up to this," Tommy blared in an angry tone.

"No, no, I didn't," Aria pleaded. "Jackie doesn't know anything about the Gallions. I promise. You're my friend. I wouldn't—"

Tommy interrupted, "You're not my friend. You're a loser! And I hate you!" Then he disconnected the call.

The screen on Aria's tBinder filled with static. She closed it and took off the earpiece. Aria sulked in her chair and stared into the night sky.

Why would Tommy say such mean and terrible things? Aria wondered. *My best friend hates me. Oh no!*

Aria's heart filled with grief. She fell across her bed and started to cry.

"I'll never ever talk to aliens," Aria promised herself. The struggle of keeping their secrets and defending their existence was too painful. "Never again."

Chapter 12
Happy Whiskers

On June 18, three days after Her Majesty's last dialogue with Aria, Queen Supreme Nashata asked Mitushi to send details of Aria's teleportation to her tDiary. The queen had pressing ship-to-home royal duties to perform instead. Mitushi ordered Peakte to join him in Holospace Five and requested LeSom's presence as interpreter. Mitushi stood in front of the Tay Com and placed his tentacles on its sides. Peakte set the Tay Com's controls for audio-to-text so that Mitushi's words would appear as a journal entry in Aria's tDiary. He signaled Mitushi to begin when ready.

"Hello, Aria. I am Mitushi, Commander Supreme of the Gallion Fleet. I send you greetings from my mother, the queen, and the crew of the superspaceship *Rama*."

"In two days, we will reach beaming intersection points above your planet."

"Mitushi," LeSom interrupted, "just say you will reach Earth's orbit in two days. The term *beaming intersection points* is way too geeky." Mitushi nodded his head, and Peakte made the edits in the transmission.

Mitushi continued, "We will initiate interdimensional molecular transformation upon the thirteenth hour of the day."

"Scratch that," LeSom advised. "Just tell her that we'll beam her up one o'clock in the afternoon. She'll go nuclear with all that *molecular transformation* stuff." Mitushi slowly nodded again, and Peakte made the needed edits. When

Mitushi was about to speak, LeSom whispered, "Think like they do. Connect with your inner youngirl."

Despite Peakte's attempt to hide his laughter, his whiskers sprang into a U. He flattened them with his tentacle tips and acted like nothing had happened.

Mitushi glared at Peakte's U-shaped whiskers and demanded, "Wipe that smirk off the top of your head. That's an order!"

LeSom moved between the quarreling Gallions and said, "Why don't we all sing *Kum Ba Ya*. It's a spiritual melody humans traditionally sing to seek inner peace. Kum ba ya, my Lord, kum ba ya!" Mitushi and Peakte glared at LeSom, whiskers flat on the left sides of their faces. LeSom sang another two lines.

Mitushi finally interrupted, "We're not singing along, you notice."

LeSom stopped immediately. Her whiskers drooped around her face.

"Perhaps some rock 'n' roll," LeSom suggested, "to give you happy whiskers." Then she shook the middle part of her body and loudly sang, "You ain't nothin' but a hound dog, cryin' all the time. You ain't—"

"Stop!" Mitushi yelled. He used his tentacle tips to force his whiskers in a U. "See, I have happy whiskers now." A moment of silence followed Mitushi's outburst. LeSom and Peakte felt very uncomfortable around a mad Mitushi. After a minute, Mitushi calmed down and suggested he finish the transmission to Aria.

"At the one o'clock afternoon hour, Aria, simply hold whatever you want to bring onto the superspaceship. My first engineer, Peakte, will . . . beam you aboard. We promise to make your stay as . . . funtastic as possible."

"Very good," LeSom whispered to Mitushi. His happy whiskers were genuine this time.

Seven minutes after Mitushi had delivered this information to Aria, a green light on the side of her tDiary started to blink. Aria noticed the light when she returned home from ballet class. The slot normally shined red when the battery was low. Aria realized the flashing green light meant the Gallions had sent her a message.

Could the aliens really exist, Aria wondered, *even though Tommy doesn't believe?*

As Aria watched the pulses of green light, she started to believe in herself and the aliens she had seen. Maybe she wasn't crazy. Maybe she wasn't weird. Maybe the Gallions were real!

Aria quickly opened her tDiary but stopped just before accessing the Gallion's message. Tommy's harsh words now echoed in her mind. She started to doubt again.

What if I am a loser? What if aliens don't exist? And if they are real, how can I trust them? What if I'm kidnapped and tortured? What if they abduct me, and I never see Mom and Dad again?

Aria lowered the lid of her tDiary and stepped away from her desk. She decided not to read the Gallions' message. Ever.

No one would believe me, anyway.

Chapter 13
Project Watchdog

The next day, Vice Admiral Albert Jennings called William into his office at Naval Air Station Oceana. Jennings handed William a folder about a top-secret government satellite technology called Project Watchdog. He explained that the Air Force had designed this new satellite to detect potentially hostile sounds in Earth's atmosphere as an early-warning security system. The first test of Project Watchdog identified unknown transmissions coming from a distant part of the Milky Way. These signals were being sent to Virginia Beach.

"Until we know the source and purpose of these message, all branches of the military in the Tidewater area are on yellow-one alert."

"Sir, what do these messages say?" William asked.

The vice admiral paused for a moment, then confided, "We're not sure, Bull's-Eye." William had been given the call sign Bull's-Eye during his freshman year at VMI based on his superb shooting skills. "We believe one part—and remember this is classified—sounds like Elvis."

"Elvis?" William blurted with a surprised look on his face.

"The hound dog song, to be exact. And no, I'm not going crazy. The last thing I need is a bunch of shrinks on base tying up everyone's time with silly psych tests."

"Can we decode any of the transmissions?" William asked, doing his best to keep a straight face.

"Our communications experts are working on it. The Hound Dog—I mean Watchdog—team lead has requested that Lieutenant Manger work with their analysts.

Elizabeth Manger, Tommy's mother, had joined the Navy SEALS after winning five Olympic medals in swimming and third-place in an international triathlon. She had lived with her military family in Russia and China most of her childhood years, learning to speak the native languages fluently without an American accent. She also had picked up German, French, Spanish, and some Italian while stationed in Europe. Elizabeth had been given the call sign "Saltine" early on in her training because she easily cracked highly encrypted communications.

William confidently replied, "I'll send Saltine to the Watchdog team lead immediately." He admired Saltine's intelligence and strength, and he felt proud to include her in this mission. Their kids being friends gave them an even deeper bond of trust.

"And Bull's-Eye, don't mention anything to Saltine about the Elvis song. If it's really there, she'll hear. We need her unbiased verification. Personally, I'm ready to call those Hound Dog—I mean Watchdog—testers a bunch of loonies."

William tried not to laugh. The whole scene—Elvis song and all—sounded like it belonged more in a science-fiction comedy than on a naval air station.

"One more thing, Bull's-Eye."

"Yes sir?"

"Ready a direct action squad just in case Project Watchdog escalates. For now, you will serve as the SEAL liaison with the Air Force, CIA, and FBI on a joint-services investigation. If Saltine finds anything dangerous in these outer-space transmissions, we will escalate to a joint-services invasion and prepare to defend ourselves. Bull's-Eye, the safety of our nation may depend on you."

That night William tossed and turned in bed. He felt anxious and stressed from the events of Project Watchdog. Elizabeth had said the transmissions were unlike any she had ever seen or heard, except for the Elvis song. They had traveled faster than the speed of light and had contained symbols not found on Earth. By the end of the day, the military was on yellow-two alert.

When William finally fell asleep, he dreamt he was on an enemy ship. He limped down a hallway lined with columns of white lights, blood oozing from his leg. When he found the central power supply, he planted a bomb large enough to blow up a ten-story building. As he was about to escape, Jackie and Aria ran down the hallway toward him.

In his dream they shouted, "Daddy, Daddy, don't!" Then the bomb exploded early, and they were all killed.

William gasped and sat up straight. Sweat covered his forehead.

Lindsay mumbled, "Another bad dream, honey?"

"Ah, yeah," William replied. He put his hand over his pounding heart and anxiously said, "I need to check on the girls."

William had had bad dreams before missions, but none of them had involved his family. Until tonight.

He quietly opened Jack's door and looked inside. Everything appeared normal, including her mild snoring. Next, William poked his head inside Aria's bedroom. He found her curled on her side in her favorite purple pajamas. A blinking green light on Aria's desk caught William's attention. He walked toward it.

Just a tDiary, William said to himself. *Perfectly harmless.*

Chapter 14
Mission Attack Dog

Aria and one of her close friends, Meredith Spheeris, played board games at Aria's home on the rainy morning of June 20. When the sky cleared two hours later, Meredith invited Aria to her house to play in the pool and sleep over that night. Lindsay agreed to the sleepover and confirmed with Mrs. Spheeris that the plans suited her as well. Aria crammed enough clothes for two days in her pink beach bag and walked with Meredith to her house.

When the girls arrived, Mrs. Spheeris—who worked in the Greek shipping business from home—explained that the sleepover wouldn't work after all. She had just received an urgent message from her boss that she had to be in New York the next day for an important meeting. Mrs. Spheeris apologized and promised the girls they could have a sleepover next week. She fed them her famous shrimp scampi for lunch and sent Aria back home.

Aria felt so disappointed. Spending time with Meredith had helped her forget the pain about fighting with Tommy. Now the loneliness crept into her heart again. Aria sulked as she slowly walked down the sidewalk with a big frown on her face.

At an intersection of two neighborhood streets, Aria lifted her head to check for traffic. Her sorrow was abruptly overshadowed by the queasy sensation she usually felt before receiving a prediction. Only this time, she envisioned herself spiraling, fast as light, toward a blue whale. Suddenly *swish*—she wasn't in Virginia anymore.

Later that afternoon, Vice Admiral Jennings told William to join him in the War Plans Room for an emergency meeting of the Joint Special Operations Command. They sat around a large table with Air Force General Peter Goforth and agents from Homeland Security, the FBI, and CIA.

"Good news and bad news," the general explained. "For the good news, the transmissions to Virginia Beach detected by Project Watchdog have ceased. No more hostile sounds have been heard. Now for the bad news." The general pointed to a large screen in the front of the room that displayed a very fuzzy picture of the *Rama*. "Shortly after the transmissions stopped, our satellites over the Pacific Ocean captured this photo of an unidentified flying object in the air." The general flipped to the next shot, which showed a grainy image of the *Rama* entering the ocean. "And then in the water."

"Our submarines tracked the UFO for fifteen yards," Jennings added. "Then the vessel disappeared from our radar off the coast of Maui. We haven't picked up a signal since."

"That's where the SEALs come in, Captain Vanir," Goforth said as he pointed to William. "You will command a squad of eight SEALs, divided into two teams, for a direct action mission. From the closest U.S. nuclear submarine, your squad will navigate our latest underwater delivery vehicles, the aqualaports, to the last known location of the UFO. Find that alien ship. Investigate, but be cautious. We don't know who or what is aboard that . . . thing. Its speed and technology surpass any jet or ship we've seen on Earth."

"General, what are our rules of engagement?" William asked.

"If you meet alien life-forms, attempt friendly contact at first. Follow diplomacy guidelines AG409. Have you been briefed on these procedures?"

"Yes, sir," William quickly responded. "I am clear on the alien contact process."

"Very good, Vanir," Goforth nodded at Jennings to continue the briefing.

"Bull's-Eye, the next part is need-to-know for your SEALs only," Jennings ordered. "Upon any failure of diplomacy, you are to lead your squad in a covert mission called Attack Dog." Jennings gave William a red folder marked *Confidential*, which contained orders and details about Attack Dog. "You are to disable the UFO and extract as many alien enemies as possible, starting with their leaders. Your squad will be secretly armed with heavy explosives to render the vessel helpless. Upon your signal, we will send additional aqualaports to transport the prisoners. Do you understand, Bull's-Eye?"

William confidently nodded his head and replied, "Sir, yes, sir!"

"Good," Jennings continued. "Next you will rendezvous with the submarine where we will begin our interrogation of the alien captives. At that point, the Air Force and FBI will examine the ETs and their UFO for input to the X-Files."

William flipped through the pages of the Attack Dog folder and said, "I've prepared my squad, sir . . . for anything. Especially close-quarter battle."

"Excellent work, Bull's-Eye. Any questions?"

William shook his head. The only thought in his mind, which he dared not share with his superior officer, was his nightmare of blowing up an alien ship while his daughters were aboard.

It was just a silly dream, William reminded himself.

An hour later William called Lindsay and told her he had to leave immediately.

"Oh, honey, not again," Lindsay complained.

William closed his eyes and took a deep breath. He knew Lindsay would get upset, and he always regretted having to say goodbye to her on the phone.

"I'm sorry, honey. This mission came up at the last minute. They need me, Lindsay. This is why I train so hard. To protect you, the girls—"

"God and country," Lindsay interrupted. "Yes, I know the routine. Train for war, fight to win, defeat our nation's enemies. Just come back to me, Will. All in one piece. No broken bones or bullet wounds this time. You hear?"

"Yes, Miss Lindsay," William said with a Southern accent to tease his wife.

"Seriously, Will, can you tell me where or—"

"You know I can't say anything. I'm sorry, Lizzy, but it's a matter of national security." Lindsay fought back tears to say, "These dang missions. I worry so much about you."

"Don't worry about me now. I have a great team. Intelligent. Highly skilled. We're the best. Focus on the girls while I'm gone. Keep everything going until I get back."

Then Lindsay started to cry. William's shoulders sank when he heard his wife's sobs.

"I love you, Lindsay. I promise I'll return. Promise. Gotta go now. Bye."

Lindsay caught her breath long enough to reply, "I love you, too. Goodbye."

When Jackie came home that evening from surfing, her mother was standing in front of the bay window that faced the naval air station. Lindsay rubbed her favorite gold locket in her fingers and watched jets fly overhead. The locket contained a small picture of William and her on their honeymoon. Lindsay didn't even look at her daughter or fuss at her when she tracked sand into the house. She just stared out the window, motionless and speechless.

Jackie dropped her beach bag on the floor when she saw her mother. She wanted to say or ask something, but couldn't find the right words. She knew the only time her mother constantly rubbed that locket was when her father had left for a mission.

Lindsay reached for a tissue from a nearby table without taking her eyes off the sky. She envisioned her husband being flown to a hostile place.

Jackie softly said, "Mom?"

Lindsay turned and faced her daughter. Tears flooded her eyes and streamed down her face.

With a quivering voice, Lindsay said, "Your dad's . . . away."

Jacqueline nodded and took a deep breath. She wanted to appear strong to help her mother, so she fought crying.

Lindsay continued, "I don't know where he's gone or when he'll be back or what he's doing. Oh, Jacqueline!" Lindsay walked across the room and hugged her daughter. Then she wept some more.

"We'll be okay, Mom. We always are. We'll get some pizza and watch CNN like we always do." Jackie took another deep breath and struggled to talk without crying. "Dad will come home. Maybe not tomorrow, but soon. He always comes home, you know that."

Lindsay released her daughter and said, "Thanks, sweetie. You're right. I need to focus on taking care of us now." Lindsay walked to the refrigerator and scanned the tBuy bar code for pizza coupons. Jacqueline followed her to the kitchen. "Oh, by the way," Lindsay said, "Aria is staying at Meredith's tonight. It will be just the two of us for pizza."

"Astro," Jacqueline said. She always enjoyed an evening free from her little sister. "Let's get a large supreme. I'm starving. Waves were great after the storm."

As Lindsay ordered the pizza, Jacqueline watched a story on CNN about a small asteroid that had crashed into the Pacific Ocean near Maui. The collision had caused the highest waves of the year, and famous surfers had gathered there to ride the big ones.

Lucky dudes, Jackie thought to herself. *Wish I were there. Some people get to have all the fun.*

Chapter 15
LeSom's Greeting

Bright lights glared in Aria's eyes as she staggered around Holospace Five, wondering what had happened to her. The hard sidewalk where she had stood now felt spongy and bouncy, like a mat in gymnastics class. The warm wind that had been blowing her auburn hair across her face quickly calmed to a whisper. The smell of salty air and sounds of jets overhead disappeared instantly. In her confusion, Aria stepped backward and bumped into something large and slick. She spun around and raised her hand to shield her eyes from the lights. Aria looked up and beheld Princess LeSom, in the golden flesh.

"Aaaahhhhh!" Aria screamed at the top of her lungs.

LeSom expected Aria to act like a sweet youngirl—friendly, courteous, and hospitable—especially since Aria had talked to the queen. Wrong. Now LeSom regretted volunteering to great Aria until Mitushi and Ora could arrive.

Aria's frightened reaction scared LeSom. She screamed as well, and her whiskers fanned out like porcupine quills.

The diplomatic relations started on the wrong foot.

For Aria, seeing the Gallions up close and personal was far scarier than viewing a small image of them in the comfort of her home. She ran away from LeSom and cried for her parents. LeSom didn't move. She still felt shocked by Aria's odd behavior.

"The youngirl's gone nuclear," LeSom muttered to herself. "I must help her find happy whiskers. But how?"

LeSom's whiskers swayed as she quickly pondered a way to show friendship to Aria. Then her whiskers parted into a U as she started to sing, "Kum ba ya, my Lord, Kum ba ya."

Unfortunately, LeSom's singing frightened Aria even more. Aria found the door of Holospace Five and banged on it.

"Help me!" Aria yelled as she frantically searched for way to open the holospace door.

LeSom realized the music wasn't giving Aria happy whiskers, so she stopped singing. In the silence, Aria started to calm down as well. LeSom remembered what the queen had told her about the peace sign Americans made with their hands.

With a soft voice LeSom calmly said, "Aria, peace."

Aria turned around and saw LeSom with two tentacle tips in the air. She still felt frightened, so she took a deep breath for her next scream.

LeSom quickly explained, "I am Princess LeliaSomona of the Gallions." Aria recognized the creature's last word. She simply exhaled instead of screaming. "The queen, my sister, sent me to greet you." Aria slowly nodded her head to acknowledge the queen's invitation to board the superspaceship. LeSom's whiskers parted into a U as she continued, "We offer you our finest hospitality. Aria Vanir, you are safe with us."

The way LeSom had said "safe" reminded Aria of how her mother had reassured her that there weren't monsters under her bed or giant sharks in the surf. Aria relaxed and looked into LeSom's lavender eyes. Something about that gentle color made Aria smile. She realized a soul connection with the Gallion princess, even though their lands were stars apart.

LeSom shook her tentacle tips to make her peace sign wiggle back and forth. Aria giggled. She raised her hand and made a peace sign as well.

Aria stood up straight like a soldier and proclaimed, "Peace from . . . planet Earth." Then she reached out and touched LeSom's tentacle tips with her fingertips. It was like touching the end of a puppy's nose. She smiled and laughed again.

The diplomatic relations had just turned friendly.

Aria covered her eyes with her hand and complained, "The lights are too bright. Can you dim them?" Aria searched around the holospace for her sunglasses, which had fallen off her face after she had been beamed aboard. She found them, but they were broken. "Ah, nuke it," Aria moaned.

LeSom's whiskers drooped. She didn't know how to dim the lights, much less fix Aria's sunglasses. Since the Gallions lived on a planet with two suns, they had adapted to more light than humans could easily tolerate. From birth, Gallions required intense brightness to see.

"I'm getting a headache," Aria whined.

LeSom picked up the sunglasses and examined them. She tried to wear them, but they were far too small.

"Manifester," LeSom ordered, "show me dark sunglasses for human youngirl." The small matrix of white-light columns glowed and buzzed. Aria squeezed her eyes shut to protect them.

A feminine voice from the machine said, "Please specify brand. Top sellers include Ray-Ban, Oakley, and Maui Jim."

"Maui Jim, please," LeSom answered. "When in Hawaii . . ." She added, "For small faces, remember." Pictures of five sunglasses appeared at the front of the holospace. LeSom reviewed them and said, "I like the first one. Aria, what's your favorite?" Aria shielded her eyes with her hands and squinted at the sunglasses. She quickly nodded her head in agreement. "First pair it is!" LeSom exclaimed.

"Would you like accessories?" the manifest machine asked. "We carry case, cleaning kit, and cord." LeSom looked at Aria, who nodded her head again.

"Please," LeSom replied.

"You have selected Maui Jim's Youth Sleuth shades with case, cleaning kit, and cord. Would you like to manifest now, or continue ordering?"

"Manifest now," LeSom said. Crystals in the manifest machine glowed and buzzed again. The sunglasses and accessories appeared on the floor in front of the holospace. LeSom gave them to Aria, who quickly put on the sunglasses.

Aria gasped and then said, "Astro fizz! Oh, thank you so much." She looked around the holospace without having to squint or hide her eyes. When Aria felt comfortable with her surroundings, she attached the cord to her sunglasses and stuffed the cleaning kit in her beach bag. Now, she focused on LeSom.

"Why are you so big?" Aria asked. "The queen was just about, oh, eight inches tall."

LeSom explained, "What you saw was just a small image of the queen projected from the Tay Com to your tDiary. Most Gallions are my size or slightly smaller. We look the same, except for different markings on our backs and below our necks. See?"

Aria stepped behind LeSom and looked at her markings. She felt wildly curious, so she reached out her hand and stroked LeSom's back. The alien's golden body felt slick, like a melting ice cube. The black parts were coarse and reminded Aria of running her hands across freshly cut grass.

Aria looked around the holospace again. She didn't find any windows to look outside.

"Where are we? You said something about Hawaii earlier. Where are you taking me?"

"Ah, yes," LeSom muttered. "My, you do have very strong ears for an alien." LeSom made a mental note to speak more softly when she didn't want Aria to hear her. "You see, Aria, we had wanted to beam you aboard the *Rama* and then hide in the Atlantic Ocean. But a funny thing happened on the way to the Bahamas. All the large landing pads in Atlantis were taken. The place was so congested from the new construction, anyway. With all these problems, Mitushi decided to fly to the Pacific Quadrant instead. Off the coast of Maui is a gateway—"

"Mitushi?" Aria interrupted. "Who's Mitushi?"

"Commander Supreme of the Gallion Fleet. Son of Queen Supreme Nashata. My nephew. He's the one who sent you the transmission two days ago. He said we'd beam you aboard at one o'clock today." Aria looked puzzled. "On your tDiary," LeSom continued. "I even translated his military mumbo jumbo into youngirl lingo. Oh, tell me you got the message!"

Aria lowered her eyes and shook her head. She glanced at her watch—eighteen minutes past one o'clock. Aria felt too ashamed to admit she had thought the Gallions were a hoax. Now she knew she had been wrong.

"Well, no wonder you went nuclear when we beamed you to the holospace. You must have been terrified."

Aria nodded and said, "Yes, and I'm sorry I screamed."

LeSom wrapped a tentacle around Aria's shoulder and softly said, "It's our little secret." Having a cool, moist tentacle on her bare shoulders felt astro whacked to Aria.

"So we're flying to Maui . . . as in Hawaii . . . as in Pearl Harbor?" Growing up as a Navy brat, Aria often knew locations by military bases.

"Close. We are flying—or rather diving—through the Pacific Ocean to the Lemurian base. Their landing pads are larger and more modern."

"Will I get to see a volcano and go to a luau? I've always wanted to dance at one of those." Aria waved her arms together and shook her hips like she was a Hawaiian hula dancer.

LeSom slowly explained, "Not exactly. You see, we've had to—"

Princess LeSom was interrupted by the door of Holospace Five opening. Mitushi marched in, followed by Ora. They stopped in front of Aria. LeSom held up two tentacles in a peace sign and motioned to Mitushi and Ora to do the same.

"Greetings, Aria Vanir. I am Mitushi, Commander Supreme of the Gallion Fleet. Welcome to the superspaceship *Rama*. We are honored to have you aboard."

Aria raised her hand to form a peace sign and timidly said, "Peace from Earth." She stretched her arm to press her fingertips against Mitushi's tentacles. They felt clammy, and Aria fought to keep a straight face.

"This is my beloved, Ora," Mitushi said as he lowered his tentacles and looked at Ora. "She serves as our ambassador supreme to Earth."

Ora looked at Aria and stated, "We wish friendship and prosperity for our peoples."

Aria touched her fingertips to Ora's tentacles. She tried to think of something mature or proper to say, but she felt so overwhelmed. Then Aria noticed Ora's large, lavender eyes. As Aria stared into them, she sensed the same calmness and safety she had experienced with LeSom.

"Friends," Aria finally replied. "And peace." She smiled because she knew she had done the best she could.

The diplomatic relations continued to blossom.

"By the way, youngirl Aria, what is that instrument covering your eyes?"

"Sunglasses!" Aria exclaimed as she pointed to her face. "Maui Jim's Youth Sleuth, to be exact. Miss LeSom manifested them for me."

LeSom explained to her nephew, "The lights on this ship are too bright for their eyes. Remember, they have just one sun."

"Ah," Mitushi replied. "I understand. Perhaps engineering can modify the brightness from our crystals for you." Mitushi touched the rim of Aria's sunglasses with his tentacle tips and observed, "Everything you see is filtered through these lenses. Hum-mmmm. Then these sunglasses see everything through your eyes as well. Fascinating."

"That's correct," Aria responded. Mitushi lowered his tentacles, but he continued to survey Aria's sunglasses. Aria was far more interested in learning about the aliens. She pointed to the Gallions and repeated their names, "Princess LeSom, Commander Supreme Mitushi, and Ambassador Supreme Ora." The Gallions nodded as Aria said their names.

Aria noticed that Mitushi was standing so close to Ora that their tentacles were touching. She remembered how Mitushi had referred to Ora as his beloved. Aria wondered if that meant wife.

"So are y'all married?" Aria asked Mitushi and Ora.

"We pledged partnership to each other in a ceremony similar to your Earth wedding," Mitushi replied. He wrapped his tentacles around the middle section of Ora's waist. His whiskers parted into a U.

"Do y'all have kids?"

Ora shook her head and said, "In Earth time we've been married for only three months. But we've known each other for ten years. We've flown many missions together, Mitushi as the commander and—"

"Ora as the ship's first shielder," Mitushi added. "We make an amazing team."

"What's a shielder?" Aria asked Ora.

"I protect the ship."

"Like, shields up?"

"Yes. I also disguise the ship so our enemies can't see us. If needed, I can stabilize the ship through wormholes, asteroid belts, and battle maneuvers."

"Astro," Aria mumbled. "So how does a Gallion put up shields?"

"We modify molecular structures the same way you mold clay. Our world is not about density, but destiny. We see something not for what it is, but for what it can be."

Aria wrinkled her forehead and shook her head. She felt quite perplexed. Ora understood Aria's confusion, so she quickly changed the subject.

"Let's go to Holospace Seven, Aria. We've recreated your home there. It looks just the way it does in Virginia Beach."

"Is Mom there? What about Dad and Jackie?"

"Not exactly," Ora slowly replied. She looked at Mitushi for guidance on what to say next. He remained silent.

"So!" LeSom exclaimed to divert Aria's attention. "What types of music do you like, Aria? I know hundreds of languages and thousands of songs. I can mimic voices and styles to near perfection."

In a sarcastic tone, Mitushi added, "And she's so humble about her talents."

Aria looked at Mitushi and said, "If you are the son of a queen, then you are a prince. Right?"

LeSom and Ora made happy whiskers. Mitushi's whiskers drooped beside his eyes. He felt embarrassed about being called a prince because he hadn't been able to pronounce that word as a Gallion toddler. It had always came out as "ince." Being teased about this speech challenge had made Mitushi despise his title. He had told everyone to refer to him as the commander supreme or son of the queen. LeSom and Ora wanted to laugh out loud whenever someone called Mitushi a prince.

LeSom whispered in Aria's ear, "He likes to be called the commander supreme or just commander for short. Let's keep it at that, okay?" Aria nodded her head. LeSom turned to Ora and asked, "Can I go with you and Aria to her room on Holospace Seven? I'd like to learn more about her music."

"Certainly," Ora responded.

"Astro!" Aria squealed. Rarely had any human adult, much less an alien princess, expressed an interest in her music. "I have three 'My Favorites' playlists on my tMuz."

Aria reached in her beach bag and pulled out her tMuz, a thumb-sized media and music player. She showed it to the three Gallions.

LeSom turned to Mitushi and asked, "Could one of your engineers build an interface from this tMuz to my whiskers? I'd like to download her songs."

"I'll send someone to Holospace Seven to look at it. Remember, this is very primitive technology."

"I got it at Christmas," Aria snapped. She felt defensive and humiliated. "They haven't even come out with the new version yet."

"It is a wonderful device," Ora calmly stated. "I'm sure it plays your music with a great deal of accuracy and clarity."

Aria smiled and nodded her head. Ora glared at Mitushi with a don't-say-that-again look on her face.

"Nice device," Mitushi mumbled, in the interest of friendly relations.

"Let's go look at your room," Ora said to Aria. She wrapped her tentacle tips around one of Aria's dainty hands. LeSom held onto Aria's other hand.

"By the way, Aria," Mitushi added, "the queen sends her gracious wishes for a pleasant journey."

Aria turned around and replied, "Thanks! So . . . when I get to meet her?"

"Soon," he replied. "Your journey of seeking the queen has just begun."

Chapter 16
Hiding the *Rama*

While Lindsay and Jackie watched the CNN story about the small asteroid that had landed near Maui, Queen Supreme Nashata summoned Mitushi to her royal suite on the *Rama*. She wanted a report on Aria and the location of their superspaceship. More importantly, she wanted to discuss defense strategies in case something . . . unfortunate . . . happened.

Mitushi told the queen about his first encounter with Aria, which was a positive interaction. He also described Aria's sunglasses and tMuz, which he wanted his engineering team to study. As far as Mitushi was concerned, Aria was ready for her next step to meet the queen in person.

"Splendid!" the queen exclaimed as she clapped her tentacles together. Her whiskers stood upright and then parted into a U. "I knew there was something most spectacular about that youngirl. Now, how is my ship?"

"We've reached the designated landing pad at Lemuria. The Lemurian High Priestess communicated her gracious pleasure at our surprise visit. She insisted you receive a new set of keys to the capital. They had to change the locks last century; too much corrosion from the salt water."

"Well, these underwater civilizations have many struggles to keep their location a secret. Tell the High Priestess I am honored to accept her invitation. I'll ask Forkana to work with Ora on the details. I quite believe Ora is turning out to be a fine ambassador. Don't you agree?"

"Absolutely, Mother. She still amazes me as our first shielder, especially her camouflage capabilities. As soon as we dived into the Pacific Ocean, Ora and the other shielders disguised the *Rama* as a pod of dolphins."

"Fascinating!" the queen exclaimed.

"The shielders then altered the disguise to a whale, which allowed us to dive undetected to Lemuria. Once we docked on the landing pad, the shielders changed the cloak into a giant coral reef covered with algae. Little fish are now swimming around us to find food and new homes."

"Brilliant ideas. But about being undetected, Mitushi. I want you to watch these tapes Arcthena showed me. She's been using Holospace Three to monitor any Earth chatter related to UFOs, aliens, transmissions, foreign ships, et cetera. Let's go into the viewing room."

The queen and Mitushi walked into an adjacent room. A manifest machine stood in the center, surrounded by comfy chairs. The queen and her son sat facing the machine.

"Manifester," the queen said, "show us tape number five of Earth military discussion, labeled Goforth." The crystals of the manifest machine glowed and buzzed. "The American satellites allowed easy surveillance of most cities on their planet. I wonder if they know how vulnerable they really are."

The manifest machine stopped glowing and buzzing. Above it appeared an image of William and Vice Admiral Jennings entering a large briefing room.

"Here we go," the queen whispered. "Pay particular attention to the one they call Bull's-Eye."

Arcthena, the queen's security handmaiden, had recorded the entire meeting between William, Jennings, and General Goforth in which they discussed transmissions to Virginia

Beach and UFO sightings near Maui. She also had taped the follow-up conversations and strategy sessions about how the SEALs had planned to search for and possibly attack the *Rama*.

"So you see, Mitushi," the queen said after reviewing the tapes with her son, "we are not quite as safe as you had expected."

Mitushi's whiskers started to droop. He didn't realize American technology could detect his ship while it traveled at low altitudes inside Earth's atmosphere.

"Sorry, Mother. I'll be more careful next time we are in the air. I'll also alert Ora and the shield team to double the protective barrier. For now, I assure you we are hidden from the humans."

"Good. Now we must remain out of sight for the sake of the Gallions and Lemurians. Besides, it's not all your fault. Somehow they even tracked my sister's Elvis impersonations. If word about that reaches the Vitcheran Wormhole, I'll be laughed off the Intergalactic Oversight Council."

"I won't let that happen, Mother."

"Thanks, son. Actually, I'm far more worried about something else."

"What's that?"

"Did you happen to notice the other name for Bull's-Eye, the officer in charge of finding and possibly destroying us?"

"Yes—Vanir. William Vanir. Is he in Aria's tribe?"

"More than that—he's Aria's father!"

Mitushi's whiskers fanned out as he asked, "You mean Aria's father and these . . . *seals* . . . could attack us?"

The queen thought for a moment and then responded, "Now why would they send such cute little animals to attack

a superior alien race like us? Just doesn't make sense."
Matushi nodded in agreement. "Anyway, we must continue
surveillance. You never know what a seal might do."

"I'll brief our security and shield teams at once. We'll go
to level two defense alert."

"Splendid," the queen replied. "Include Arcthena. She
knows the most about the Americans' plans."

"Certainly. Mother, perhaps William Vanir and his seals
will accept us as Aria did."

"From my studies of Earth culture, that isn't likely to
happen. Governments send those who have been trained to
kill. We must be prepared. Absolutely prepared. Do not
believe for an instant that the humans who come for us will
treat us with the kindness and curiosity that Aria has shown.
She is a unique individual with a fascinating destiny."

Chapter 17
Missing Aria

Lindsay spent most of Wednesday morning, June 21, on the phone with family and close friends. She told them William had left for a mission. By now they knew not to ask where and for what reason. After lunch and an afternoon nap, Lindsay felt much better. Then she looked around the house and asked herself, *Where is Aria?*

Lindsay called Meredith's mother, but no one was home. She drove to Meredith's house on her way to pick up Jackie from karate practice. No sign of Aria. Meredith, staying at the neighbor's house until her mother returned from New York, walked over when she saw Mrs. Vanir's car.

"Good afternoon, Meredith. Hope you and Aria had fun during your sleep over. I'm here to take Aria home. Can you go get her?"

"She walked home yesterday after lunch," Meredith replied. "Mom had to go to New York, so Aria couldn't stay last night. Didn't Aria tell you?"

Lindsay huffed and said, "Seriously, Meredith. I know you girls like to have fun, but this isn't a good time to joke with me." Lindsay got out of the car and started walking to the front door. "Aria! Time to go!"

The neighbors hosting Meredith came outside and met Lindsay on the steps of the Spheeris's home. They told Lindsay that they, too, had watched Aria walk down the street yesterday, shortly before one o'clock.

"This can't be happening!" Lindsay exclaimed. She put her hands on her hips and demanded, "There must be a mistake. Meredith, why didn't your mother tell me that Aria had left early? Why didn't someone check to make sure that Aria had made it home? Why didn't—" Lindsay covered her mouth with her hand before she yelled something she'd regret later. Her eyes swelled with tears. "My little girl is missing!"

The neighbors consoled Lindsay and advised her to call the police. An officer suggested she file a missing minor's report. Lindsay frantically picked up Jackie and drove them to the police station.

"I can't believe this is happening to me," Lindsay repeated over and over while the officer gathered details about Aria's last known whereabouts. Lindsay did the best she could to answer the officer's questions while crying, often asking Jackie to finish her sentences.

When Lindsay and Jackie arrived home, Lindsay sat on the porch swing and stared into the distance. She wondered where William was when she needed him the most.

Jackie searched for Aria in their bedrooms. She knew it was a silly attempt to find her little sister, but she needed to do something. Anything. While Jackie looked under her bed, she remembered the night Aria came to her room and thanked her for beating up Eric.

Jackie recalled her promise to her little sister: "I'll always protect you. Promise. We Vanir girls have to stick together."

Jackie stood up tall and proud like a SEAL, put her hands on her hips, and glared at her reflection in her dresser mirror.

"Go find your sister," Jackie grunted to herself. "Gather intel. Devise a plan. Force the enemy to disclose her location. You made a promise to protect her. Now do it! Go, go, go!"

Jackie sprang into action. First, she called Meredith and interrogated her until she started to cry. Then Jackie contacted the neighbor and questioned her until she threatened to call the police.

"I'm getting nowhere fast," Jackie mumbled to herself. She looked out her window and wondered what to do next. At that instant, Tommy was riding his scootercycle down the sidewalk near the Vanir house. He usually waved or stopped to talk to Aria. Today he just acted like strangers lived there.

Jackie ran outside, chased Tommy, and then tackled him to the ground. Despite Tommy's kicking and screaming, Jackie dragged him inside the house. She used duct tape to tie him to one of the chairs at Aria's Hospitality Station. Jackie grabbed a flashlight and sat in the other chair.

"Untie me!" Tommy demanded. "I'm telling my mom."

"Who reports to my dad. You don't stand a chance, Shrimp Bait. Might as well tell me what I want to know."

Jackie had given Tommy the nickname Shrimp Bait because he was a scrawny kid with reddish-brown hair who reminded her of Forrest Gump. Tommy despised being called Shrimp Bait. He never really understood how sweet Aria could have such a devilish sister.

"What do you want?" Tommy moaned as he tried to free his wrists from the duct tape.

Jackie shined the flashlight in Tommy's eyes and sternly asked, "Tell me the exact location of Aria Vanir."

"I don't know!" Tommy wailed. "This is a stupid game. Let me go, Dog Breath!"

Tommy's customary insult didn't interfere with Jackie's interrogation. "When was the last time you saw Aria?"

"When she told me about those stupid aliens."

"Huh?" Jackie uttered, confused.

"A couple of days ago, when we went to the beach. We built sandcastles. You surfed at the pier. We all went home. Don't you remember?"

"But then you came over later that night, right?"

"Yeah, so?" Tommy replied. He continued to wiggle in his chair as he frantically fought the duct tape.

"So . . . what happened?" Jackie moved the flashlight closer to Tommy's eyes. "Did y'all talk about running away?"

"Negative, Dog Breath. She told me about some stupid aliens who had contacted her. They left a message for her in that sissy tDiary. That's all. Now let me go!"

"You had better come up with a better story than that, Shrimp Bait."

"That's all I know. And my brother thinks your hoax thing with the aliens is a big, fat lie. You can't fool us, Dog Breath."

Jackie turned off her flashlight and sat back in her chair. She was just playing with the duct tape and questioning, but Tommy's hostile attitude toward Aria surprised Jackie. She needed to gather more intel.

"Why are you extramad at Aria? Y'all are almost like . . . kissing cousins."

"Yuck, no!" Tommy exclaimed. He fought to free himself but almost toppled to the floor. Jackie roared with laughter. Tommy's face turned beet red from anger and humiliation. He blared, "I'm extramad at you and Aria for lying to me about the aliens. Everyone knows they're not real. Even the ones who send messages to Aria's tDiary."

Jackie slowly stopped laughing. She looked at Aria's tDiary and then at Tommy.

"So exactly what did Aria say about the aliens in her tDiary?"

"Let me go, and I'll tell you."

Jackie again shined the flashlight in Tommy's eyes and calmly said, "Tell me what I want to know, and I'll let you go. Now, what did Aria say about the aliens in her tDiary?"

Tommy told Jackie what he had remembered about the Gallions, Queen Supreme Nashata, and her message to Aria. He explained that Aria had invited these aliens to Virginia Beach, and now they wanted to beam Aria aboard a superspaceship that looked like a big whale.

"I thought you knew about all that," Tommy said at the end of his explanation. "I thought you and Aria were lying to me, just to be mean."

"Aria is such a wimp when it comes to lying. Trust me. I'm her sister. And if I'm going to be mean to you, it wouldn't be over something as whacked as alien messages. That's so retro."

"So if you didn't know about the alien messages," Tommy said slowly, "and no one knows where Aria is . . ."

Jackie leaned close to Tommy and warned, "Don't even go there."

"Dude, the Gallions are here!"

Chapter 18
Finding the Gallions

William checked the navigation controls on his underwater aqualaport, which he had just ejected from the U.S. submarine that was patrolling the Hawaiian Islands. His SEAL Alpha Team—Elizabeth "Saltine" Manger, Hammer, and Mars—reported that their stations were online and fully operational. William gave a go signal for Lieutenant Commander Christopher "Dishtowel" Ragg to launch his aqualaport. Three minutes later, Dishtowel's Bravo Team—Ringer, Toothpick, and Tumbleweed—affirmed their stations were ready for action. William led his squad in their aqualaports through the Pacific Ocean to hunt for the missing UFO.

Meanwhile, on the *Rama*, Mitushi had learned from Arcthena that the American government was planning to send sea-air-land teams, not animal seals, to investigate and possibly attack the Gallions. They used records from the Gallery of Worlds to study tactics and strategies used by these SEALs. Mitushi ordered his crew to transform Holospace Two into a secure holding area in case the SEALs discovered the location of the *Rama*.

The Gallion security teams had been monitoring the U.S. submarine when the two aqualaports were dispatched. Although the aqualaports were miles away and posed no immediate threat, the Gallions didn't want to risk conflict in the Lemurian waters. Mitushi decided to bring the battle inside one of his holospaces.

"Prepare the shields for a perimeter defense array," Mitushi told Ora in Holospace Two. He had spoken to her in the no-nonsense tone he used when his ship faced a threat. Ora had grown accustomed to his gruff commands, so she didn't mind. She understood he was the authority at that moment. Ora also knew Mitushi's voice and style would soften when the danger passed and they were alone.

Ora and her four shielders formed a large circle around Holospace Two. They stretched their tentacles and locked onto one another like a family joining hands to pray before supper. Ora touched a green crystal attached to her right tentacle, generating a defense screen through herself and the other shielders.

"Complete, Commander," Ora answered in the strong voice she used when the ship was in a critical situation.

Mitushi stood outside the shielders' protective circle and touched a light-blue crystal attached to his right tentacle. He used this to communicate with other parts of his superspaceship.

"First Teleporter, are you ready?" Mitushi asked.

"Yes, Commander," First Teleporter Marta replied.

"First Engineer, what's our status on dimming the lights?"

Peakte reported, "I've modified the brightness of the energy base output to human-eye sensitivity, while maintaining enough light for us. Indeed, everyone will be able to see."

"First Healer, are you prepared for causalities—especially human?"

"Ready, Commander Supreme," First Healer Gauzette answered.

"Excellent work, leaders. First Invader, we are ready for you and your team now," Mitushi announced.

Fifteen Gallions, larger than the others, swiftly entered Holospace Two and formed a circle around the shielders. Including Mitushi, there were sixteen Gallions outside of the defense array. Mitushi stood at the head of the circle with Ora in front of him to his left and the First Invader directly on his right.

"Reporting for duty," First Invader Butch announced.

"We don't expect an offensive attack," Mitushi explained to Butch. "But we can't compromise our shielders, the queen, this vessel, the Lemurians, and especially . . . the youngirl. No harm must come to her. Do you understand?"

"Absolutely, Commander."

Mitushi slowly surveyed the holospace. He wanted to ensure everything was in place and everyone was ready. This time, he touched the light-blue crystal on his right tentacle to communicate with his entire crew.

"Attention all hands, commence first alert. I repeat, first alert."

Aria, in her replicated bedroom on Holospace Seven, panicked when she heard Mitushi's order. She ran inside her closet and hid behind her long winter coat. Princess LeSom, who had been talking to Aria about the differences between human and Gallion guys, knew what was happening in Holospace Two.

Mitushi had briefed LeSom on his military intent. He had asked her to guard Aria and keep her safe. Mitushi also had ordered LeSom to say nothing to Aria about her father or the other SEALs.

"Mitushi runs these first alerts all the time," LeSom explained. "It's really more of a . . . drill . . . than any true problem. Don't be scared, Aria. You are such a brave youngirl."

LeSom pushed sweaters aside to sit on the closet floor near Aria. She tried to look at Aria's face, but Aria had surrounded herself with her coat.

"Close the closet door," Aria snapped. "That way they won't find us." She shook so hard her coat quivered. It was a tight fit, but LeSom managed to close the closet door with her and Aria inside. "I feel better now," Aria said. "Thanks."

"Me, too," LeSom replied. "Remember, it's just a drill."

Back in Holospace Two, Mitushi ordered, "First Teleporter, lock onto the two aqualaports and the SEALs inside. Tell me when you've secured their DNA signatures."

Ten seconds later the first teleporter, Marta, replied, "We've locked onto aqualaports and SEALs, Commander. Ready on your mark."

Mitushi took a deep breath and then ordered, "Teleport!"

That instant, bright lights surrounded the aqualaports. The small ships moved so rapidly that the crew fell back in their seats.

William gain his balance and blared, "Saltine, what's out there! What do you hear?"

"I'm using the scanners from Project Watchdog, Captain," she swiftly replied. "The signal is jammed, sir."

William yelled into his port-to-port earpiece, "Dishtowel, report!"

"White lights, Captain," Dishtowel frantically replied. He struggled to slow down his aqualaport. "Navigation locked. All sensors down. We've lost control and—"

The aqualaports stopped, and the lights faded. Water drained off the shells of the aqualaports onto a squishy floor. The SEALs grabbed their guns and gathered as closely as possible to the main viewing panes.

They had found their aliens.

Chapter 19
The Attack

Inside his aqualaport, William pressed a button on the control panel and said, "Bee One to Hive. Bee One to Hive. We've made contact with flower and have pollen in sight. All bees inside flower. I repeat. All bees inside flower." That was his code to the submarine that all the aqualaports were inside the superspaceship with the aliens. "Do you read, Hive?"

No response. No buzz. No static. William's message had not been relayed to the submarine.

"Bee Two, do you have communication with Hive? I repeat, do you have communication with Hive?"

No response. No buzz. No static. The aqualaports had lost contact with each other as well.

"SEALs," William said as he motioned for them to join him in the back of the aqualaport. "This is initial contact with an alien race. Remember: First, we attempt friendly diplomacy. If that fails, I'll give the signal to execute Mission Attack Dog. You're trained. You're ready. Let's go!"

William looked out the side viewing panes of his aqualaport. He caught the attention of Dishtowel in his aqualaport. William signaled him to follow his lead and secure the surroundings.

The SEALs gathered their weapons, left their aqualaports, and stepped onto the soft floor of Holospace Two. William and Dishtowel walked in front. The others followed in formation, guns ready.

William signaled the SEALs to stop. Nothing in their training or adventure movies had prepared them properly for their first alien encounter. Seeing in person the large, golden creatures with lavender eyes and whiskers was odd enough. Facing an enemy without arms added to the peculiarity.

"Shields up and stable?" Mitushi whispered to Ora.

Ora kept her eye on the aqualaports as she answered, "Yes, Commander. Shields are ready for anything."

"You may proceed with communication, Ambassador," Mitushi said to Ora. His whiskers slightly parted into a U. He felt proud of his beloved and her new role. Mitushi also hoped his introduction to adult humans would go as well as his first experience with Aria.

Ora stepped forward. As she did, the other shielders moved inward to maintain their strong defense.

"I am Ora, ambassador supreme of the Gallions from planet Vitchera. We offer you greetings of peace." Ora bowed her head as a sign of respect and welcome.

William took three steps toward Ora. The other SEALs followed and formed rows behind him. The ones in the back turned around to protect the others. They all held laser guns, ready to fire upon William's signal. William puffed out his chest and raised his head to speak with daring authority.

"I am Captain William Vanir of the United States Navy on Earth. Please explain your presence in our country."

Mitushi stepped forward and announced, "I am Mitushi, Commander Supreme of the Gallion Fleet. We are here on a diplomatic journey. We mean you no harm. Welcome to the superspaceship *Rama XI*."

William and Mitushi stared at each other. William knew he was at a disadvantage. Fewer men. Strange location. Inferior technology. Yet he wanted to appear strong and confident in front of the Gallion commander. William had faced many enemies in worse conditions. But none of them had been aliens.

William sternly asked, "Why are you here? Which governments have you contacted?" These were standard questions to ask according to Alien Diplomacy Guideline AG409.

Mitushi replied, "We are here to establish diplomatic relations. You are the first military officers to address us. We intentionally did not contact any Earth governments. We are not concerned with them."

William felt suspicious when he heard Mitushi's last sentence. He looked around the holospace again to determine offense and defense strategies in case he had to initiate Mission Attack Dog. Something familiar caught William's attention—the columns of white lights that lined the holospace.

Where have I seen those before? William asked himself. He stared at one of the columns until he remembered the nightmare he had had about blowing up a spaceship while his daughters were on board. The scene caused William to feel anxious and doubt the Gallions' diplomatic intentions. He made a gesture with his arm to send a signal of yellow alert to the other SEALs.

"If you aren't concerned with our governments," William slowly said in a deep tone, "then who does concern you?"

Mitushi and the queen had agreed to keep Aria's presence on the *Rama* a secret for now. They didn't know how the SEALs, especially William, would react if they knew the Gallions had beamed the youngirl aboard. The queen wanted to speak with Aria personally, but it wasn't time for them to meet yet. Mitushi decided to change the subject.

"Captain Vanir, we've prepared a hospitality suite for you and your crew. You will be treated as our guests. We are a peaceful species. As you see, we have no need for . . . guns." Mitushi and Ora lifted their tentacles. "Please, disarm yourselves, and we will teleport you to the suite."

William felt too suspicious to give up his laser gun and other weapons. His teams noticed that he held his gun tightly, so they followed his lead.

"Perhaps Ambassador Ora can come with us to . . . establish diplomatic relations with our leaders."

"That won't work," Mitushi snapped. The threat caused his whiskers to fan out like porcupine quills.

"I serve aboard my ship," Ora gently explained. She wanted to turn the conversation to a more hospitable tone. "You are welcome to feast with us, Captain. The Gallions and Americans have much to learn about each other. For our own safety, we must ask you to put down your weapons."

Everything in William's military training told him to negotiate and not give up his defense. His orders were to capture the aliens, not be captured by them.

"Perhaps other . . . Gallions . . . can join us for a feast with our leaders," William suggested.

"That won't be possible," Mitushi quickly replied. "My crew stays aboard the *Rama*. Period."

William scanned the circle of Gallions. None of them held any weapons. None of them moved into a fighting position. They all stood very still.

Perhaps they are peaceful, William thought to himself. *Then again, why are they so anxious to disarm us?*

The U.S. Alien Diplomacy Guidelines stated to return to designated destination when backup was needed or relations couldn't proceed. William believed his squad was at that point.

So William demanded, "Likewise, my squad and I must return to our ship," William demanded. He signaled his teams to move backward and take shelter in the aqualaports. They started to retreat.

From studying SEAL strategies, Mitushi knew that they were trained to retreat if needed and then attack again with reinforcements. He didn't want a larger military force aboard the *Rama*. He needed to contain the situation yet remain friendly.

Mitushi raised his tentacle and said, "Captain, wait. Our sensors indicate that your aqualaports were damaged during teleportation. They won't start. Please join us for a feast while our engineers repair them."

"No one touches our ports!" William warned.

The SEAL closest to an aqualaport stepped inside, still ready to fire if needed. The others were seconds behind.

"You must not leave," Mitushi exclaimed to the SEALs. He quickly whispered to Butch, "Secure the guests—immediately."

The SEALs' boots stuck to the holospace floor like magnets. Even the ones who had started to climb the steps of the aqualaports fell to the wet floor and stayed there. Immobile. The SEALs had never experience this technology in training or the field. They struggled to fight in this circumstance.

"Release us!" William demanded. He pointed his laser gun in the direction of Mitushi and Ora. The other SEALs raised their guns and prepared to fire as well. "Immediately!"

"Secure guns," Mitushi whispered to Butch.

The fifteen invaders stretched their tentacles toward the SEALs to grab their guns. The SEALs automatically engaged in hand-to-tentacle combat maneuvers to keep their weapons. In the midst of this struggle, Hammer's gun accidentally fired twice and hit William in the back of his right thigh. He thought the Gallions had attacked him, so he decided to initiate Mission Attack Dog.

William screamed, "Execute Attack Dog. I repeat, execute Attack Dog!" Then he fell and grabbed another gun from his belt. He wanted to crawl for cover, but he remained stuck to the floor.

Mitushi ordered, "Retract!" The invaders brought their tentacles close to their bodies, behind the shielders. "Shields at full force."

The SEALs fired at the Gallions, but the aliens didn't go down or run for cover. They didn't even flinch. The shielders' defense array blocked all the laser beams and bullets. They merely bounced off the invisible shield like smooth stones skipping across a calm lake. The bullets started to ricochet and hit the SEALs. Several of them screamed as blood gushed from their bodies.

"Set shield to absorb," Mitushi quickly demanded. Ora and the other shielders instantly rearranged the molecular structure of the shield so it absorbed the bullets instead of deflecting them. The ammunition now floated in the air in front of the shielders instead of bouncing back to the SEALs. This gave Mitushi an idea.

"Shielders, absorb all weapons," Mitushi yelled above the sounds of gunfire. "Leave only humans and aqualaports on deck." The SEALs' guns, grenades, knives, and other weapons were pulled from their bodies and flung through the air to the shield. Mitushi quickly tapped the light-blue crystal in his right tentacle and ordered, "First Teleporter, move humans to Healing Quadrant.

Marta answered, "Under way, Commander."

"First Healer, prepare your team for human casualties," Mitushi instructed. "Mostly bullet and laser wounds."

Gauzette confirmed, "They will be easy to repair, Commander."

"I hope so," Mitushi mumbled.

Mitushi gazed at the puddles of water on the floor. Red lines of blood flowed into them and spread in different directions. It reminded him of veins in a human body and how vulnerable men and women are to the weapons mankind had designed.

"I certainly hope so."

Chapter 20
Through Aria's Eyes

In the safety of Holospace Seven, which still resembled Aria Vanir's home, Peakte and LeSom presented Aria with a new pair of sunglasses. Peakte explained they were like the other pair, but more advanced because his team had added automated dimming capability. Aria loved them because they had two purple streaks on the top and sides.

"Mitushi wants to take you on a tour of the *Rama*," Peakte announced. "We've modified the brightness of the energy-base output to human-eye sensitivity in certain quadrants."

"Pardon?" Aria said while she stared at herself in her dresser mirror. "What does that mean?"

"Some areas of the superspaceship," LeSom explained, "are now darker than others so you can see more easily."

"Darker, indeed," Peakte added. His tentacles wiggled nervously. This was the first time he had presented one of his team's inventions to a human. He wanted to make a good impression. "In addition, an underlying layer of energy exposes subdimensional waves that only the Gallion eyes can absorb."

"Say what?" Aria blurted.

LeSom interpreted, "Even though the quadrant is darker, the Gallions can still see as we normally do."

"Indeed, indeed," Peakte added.

"By the way, humanfriend," LeSom said, "you look spicy splash in those sunglasses."

"You think, galfriend?" Aria asked for confirmation. She liked the nicknames LeSom had made up for them.

"So def," LeSom replied. "The purple stripes complement your auburn hair. You should wear those shades all the time."

Peakte spoke up, "Indeed, indeed you can, Miss Vanir." His tentacles continued to tremble. "As I mentioned before, they have automated dimming capability. When you go into the quadrants with lower lights, your dark lenses instantly soften to a faint shade of gray. I even added hints of lavender with the gray to match the purple stripes on the rim."

"Astro!" Aria exclaimed to Peakte. "Thank you so, so much!"

"It is my honor indeed, Miss Vanir."

"When do I get to see the ship?" Aria inquired.

"Soon indeed, Miss Vanir," Peakte replied. "Mitushi will come for you when he is ready. First we have additional . . . preparations."

On Naval Air Station Oceana in Virginia Beach, Ensign Jacob "Headrock" Marshall thought he heard voices while taking inventory in the storage and disposal center. He knew he was the only one assigned to that area, which was where the Navy kept broken equipment until the mechanics had time to repair them. The voices weren't familiar to Marshall, and they definitely didn't sound military. At first he guessed they were street punks who had broken into the center to steal whatever was valuable enough to sell on the black market. He pulled his gun and slowly made his way toward the noise.

As Marshall approached the noises, he noticed lights coming from the same direction. The scene reminded him of going from his kitchen to the den in the dark when only the tHTV was on.

"Freeze!" Marshall yelled when he reached the lights and voices. The noises didn't stop. He paused and slowly lowered his weapon. The threat was just an old plasma television that had been used in one of the briefing rooms years ago.

Marshall took a deep breath and closed his eyes for a moment. He wasn't used to so much excitement in the storage and disposal center. When he opened his eyes, he watched the entertaining show.

The setting was a girl's bedroom. A tall, golden creature named Princess LeSom—who had lavender eyes, tentacles, and a head full of whiskers—was talking to someone named Aria Vanir. She was off-camera, so Marshall never saw her. In this episode, Aria was pestering LeSom about taking a tour of something called the *Rama*.

After watching the show about Aria Vanir for fifteen minutes, Marshall pressed the power button to turn off the TV. However, the scene kept playing. Marshall assumed the button was defective and looked for the cord to disconnect the TV. The cord wasn't even plugged into an outlet.

"What the . . .?" Marshall mumbled as he rolled the TV on its cart into a spacious aisle. He spent half an hour trying to figure out how to turn off the darn thing. The more buttons he pressed and wires he crossed, the more frustrated he became.

Finally Marshall put his hands on his hip and said, "I'm so nuked!"

Back on the *Rama*, the queen had just returned from receiving the new keys to the Lemurian capital. She called for

Mitushi and Ora to join her in the royal suite. They walked in with U-shaped whiskers.

"Good news, I presume?" the queen said. She signaled for Arcthena to join them.

"Yes, Mother. Aria's new sunglasses are transmitting perfectly to Captain Vanir's government in Virginia Beach."

The queen clapped her tentacles together and exclaimed, "Wonderful! Quite wonderful. Now has that Goforth fellow seen us yet?"

"No, Your Majesty," Ora answered. "Presently only a junior officer has found the media rectangle, which the humans call a plasma TV. He has been watching LeSom mostly."

The queen's whiskers drooped as she mumbled, "Let's hope she doesn't sing Elvis again."

"Mostly LeSom has been singing and dancing to a type of music Aria enjoys, called revorock," Ora explained. "The two have bonded almost like . . . sisters . . . Your Majesty. They call each other 'humanfriend' and 'galfriend.'"

"Splendid!" the queen exclaimed. "Which is why I wanted to show who we are to the human race through the eyes of an American youngirl who has accepted us. Quite splendid."

"Your Majesty, we are recording all transmissions between the sunglasses and the media rectangle," Arcthena reported, "as well as the government's reactions to what they watch. I've been reviewing the footage and will alert you to critical situations."

"Superb!"

Ora asked, "Are we ready, Your Majesty, for the next step?"

"Perhaps. How are the SEALs?"

In the Healing Quadrant of the *Rama*, Elizabeth awoke from a peaceful sleep in her hammock. Thinking she was in her king-size bed at home, she rolled twice to the right to sleep on her stomach. Only she landed face-down in the sand.

Elizabeth spat sand out of her mouth and mumbled, "What the . . .?" She shielded her eyes from the bright lights and cautiously surveyed her surroundings.

In the distance, a waterfall cascaded thirty feet into a clear lagoon. Smooth, black stones formed a boundary at the water's edge. Huge ferns and tropical plants grew around the waterfall and lagoon. A wide path of sand led from the waterfall to a clearing where Elizabeth had been sleeping. Coconut trees, banana trees, and bushes with three different types of berries grew on either side of this path. Eight hammocks stretched between the largest coconut trees.

For a moment, Elizabeth thought she had died in the UFO and had gone to a tropical paradise in heaven. The cream-colored sand felt soft under her fingers, not coarse like the beach back home. The air smelled fresh and pure. The sky looked perfectly clear.

Elizabeth took a big breath to fill her lungs with the delightful air. She felt ten years younger.

Wait, my heart is still beating, Elizabeth thought. *I can't be dead.*

Elizabeth placed her hand over the center of her chest. There she felt bare skin instead of the SEAL wetsuit she'd had on in the aqualaport. Elizabeth looked down and realized she was wearing a spaghetti-strap muumuu covered with bright flowers.

"Good God, I'm in a dress!"

Elizabeth's outburst woke Dishtowel, who had been sleeping in one of the hammocks.

"Wha—?" Dishtowel muttered. He rolled over in his hammock and faced Elizabeth. "Dang, Saltine, you look good. Who's throwing the party?"

"Get a grip, Dishtowel," Elizabeth angrily whispered to him. "Do you know our location?"

Dishtowel looked around and then replied, "Maui? Maybe we drifted and wrecked on one of the South Pacific islands. The sunlight certainly is intense enough to be near the equator."

"Then why are you wearing that whacked Hawaiian shirt and snoozing in a hammock?"

Dishtowel glanced at his colorful shirt and khaki shorts. "Nice threads, don't you think?"

"Negative," Elizabeth sternly answered. "I think we're prisoners. Don't you remember shooting at the Gallions?"

Dishtowel nodded, "Yeah, I got shot in the shoulder, right here." He raised his sleeve and pointed to where he had been wounded. There was no bleeding or scar. Even the tattoo looked normal. "I swear, Saltine, I felt the sting of a bullet right in my rotator cuff. Swear!"

"Save it for that nurse you like back at base. I injured my ankle when our boots got stuck to the floor, and then I took a laser blast to my right calf."

Dishtowel leaned over in his hammock and said, "Show me."

Elizabeth raised her dress to her knees. No blood or wound in sight. She started to walk toward Dishtowel's hammock, expecting to limp from a broken ankle. Instead, both feet were strong and healthy. She didn't hobble a bit.

Elizabeth whispered, "Something's very, very wrong with this place. We need to wake our teams and carefully search for Bull's-Eye." She frantically looked right and left. "The enemy could be watching us."

Dishtowel nodded. He and Elizabeth went to the other hammocks and woke up their teammates. All of them wore colorful island clothing. None of them showed any signs of injury. In fact, they all agreed they felt stronger than ever. They complained about just one thing—squinting from the brilliant sunlight.

"Bull's-Eye is missing," Dishtowel said after taking a headcount. "Perhaps he—"

That instant, the door of the Healing Quadrant opened. Ora and two of her best shielders entered.

The shielders had formed a protective barrier around themselves before they had stepped inside. They didn't know how the humans would react to their presence.

When the SEALs saw the aliens, they instinctively ran for cover behind the largest trees. They reached for their guns and knives to protect themselves. However, they had no weapons.

"Greetings, humans. Please allow me to reintroduce myself. I am Ora, Ambassador Supreme for the Gallions. We offer you peace and an opportunity for friendship between our nations."

The Gallions raised their tentacles to form peace signs.

"They must think we're nuts," Dishtowel cautiously whispered to a member of his team.

"We believe you were . . . misinformed about us," Ora replied. "We think the people of Earth fear too much about themselves and everything around them. Especially what is odd or new. How can you possibly explore, learn, and evolve as a species when you hide from those who seek peaceful coexistence with you?"

"You tried to kill us," Dishtowel yelled, "and you've captured our leader." He had spoken more loudly so all the SEALs could hear him. With William gone, Dishtowel was next-in-charge. All the SEALs peered around their trees to make eye contact with Dishtowel. He used hand signals to tell them to surrounded the Gallions.

"On the contrary, we defended ourselves against your attack. Your own weapons injured you. Our healers repaired the damage to your bodies. Most effectively, I see, as you move about so quickly."

Dishtowel bolted to the tree closest to the Gallions. He signaled for his team to hide behind bushes near him. His plan was to charge the Gallions from the right, while Saltine and her teammates attacked them from the left.

"Where's Captain Vanir?" Dishtowel shouted to disguise the noise his team made as they moved.

"He's still . . . recovering. But someone else prepares to meet you."

Chapter 21
Acceptance

Ora touched the tip of a clear crystal in her right tentacle, which sent an alert to Mitushi that the SEALs were ready. Mitushi, Butch, and a second invader escorted Aria from Holospace Seven to the Healing Quadrant. For Aria, this was more exciting than Christmas when both her parents were home. She skipped up and down the corridors and asked dozens of questions. Other Gallions who passed by her raised their tentacle tips to form peace signs. Aria said howdy to all of them while she waved or made the peace sign with her fingers. Finally the group stopped at the entrance of the Healing Quadrant.

"How do those sunglasses fit, Aria?" Mitushi asked while he adjusted Aria's shades on her face. He wanted to ensure the Navy officials witnessed what was about to happen.

"Just fine, Mitushi. I think they're spicy splash. I love wearing them. They feel almost . . . magical."

"I'll give your compliments to Peakte."

"What's in here?" Aria asked as she tapped her knuckles on the door.

"This is our Healing Quadrant, Aria, where we—"

"Is it like the infirmary or doctor's office?"

"Yes, in that the intent is to help people feel better."

"I'm not sick," Aria firmly stated, "and I don't want to catch anything."

"We know you are quite healthy. You see, Aria, this room in the Healing Quadrant is for patients who have recovered from their injuries or diseases. They are given time to rest in the most relaxing and fun place possible before they go back to work."

"Sounds astro!"

"Er, yes. Astro. Now Aria, we have a surprise for you behind these doors. Don't be shocked. Just . . . go with the flow."

Aria eagerly bounced in place and clapped her hands together. She couldn't wait to see her surprise.

The doors of the Healing Quadrant opened. Aria ran inside, followed by Mitushi and his two invaders. Aria ran up to Ora and squeezed her tentacle tips to say hello.

"What's the surprise?" Aria blurted to Ora. She noticed her sunglasses turned darker to adjust for the additional light. Aria looked around and exclaimed, "Astro fizz, check out this beach. Did you manifest Hawaii in here?"

Elizabeth, still hiding behind a tree, recognized Aria's voice. Elizabeth was too far from Dishtowel to tell him that Aria was William's daughter, so she signaled Dishtowel that she was ready to rush the Gallions.

Dishtowel nodded and ordered, "Go, go, go!"

The seven SEALs charged toward the Gallions. Elizabeth ran directly for Aria and prepared to save her from Ora. The SEALs hit the shielders' invisible, protective barrier and tumbled to the sand.

Mitushi touched a light-blue crystal attached to his right tentacle and said, "Gauzette, we need assistance for seven SEALs in the Healing Quadrant. Mostly head and shoulder injuries from charging into the shield."

"Three healers are on the way, Commander."

Aria darted toward Elizabeth. Ora quickly adjusted the shield to allow the youngirl to pass.

"Miss Elizabeth, Miss Elizabeth," Aria hurriedly said, "are you hurt?" Aria sat beside Elizabeth and gently touched her arm. "Why did you run at the Gallions like that? Did they beam you aboard, too? Astro!" Then Aria leaned to Elizabeth's ear and whispered, "Is Tommy here? He didn't believe me when I told him about the Gallions."

Elizabeth had a splitting headache and felt nauseated. Still, she grabbed Aria's arm and tried to dash back to the trees for cover.

"I'll save you," Elizabeth sluggishly said. She felt queasy when she tried to stand and lift Aria.

"From what?" Aria asked. "I'm not in danger."

Three Gallion healers entered the room. They placed themselves between the shielders for protection and then stretched their tentacles to the seven SEALs.

Colored lights—green, blue, gold, and purple— radiated from the healers' tentacles and surrounded the SEALs. Next, the healers made high-pitched tones with their whiskers. The SEALs slowly fell asleep on the sand. Finally the healers touched their tentacle tips to the SEALs' heads and feet. Aria held Elizabeth's hand the whole time and sensed the calming energy from the healers.

After three minutes, the healers retracted their tentacles. The SEALs woke up and looked at each other.

"How do you feel?" Aria asked Elizabeth.

"Fine, fine," Elizabeth responded. She jumped up and hoisted Aria over her shoulders without any problem.

Aria pleaded, "The Gallions healed y'all. I saw everything. I tried to tell you . . . they're our friends!"

All of Elizabeth's military training told her to find a weapon—stick, rock, anything—and run for cover to protect

Aria. Even with her life. Then, something in Elizabeth's heart allowed an intuitive belief that, perhaps, Aria was right. If the Gallions had intended harm, then Aria and the SEALs would be in a prison. Or dead. Maybe they weren't in danger. Perhaps there was a greater purpose in this introduction to an alien race. Elizabeth gently lowered Aria to the ground.

"Trust me on his one," Elizabeth whispered to Dishtowel. "Let me speak with them."

Back in the storage and disposal center, Marshall nearly hyperventilated as he nervously alerted his commanding officer on his tRad.

"Lieutenant Dewey, sir, it's Headrock. SE-SEALs and a little girl with aliens. Th-they . . . they . . ."

"Slow down, Headrock. Get a grip. Over."

"Sir, a broken plasma TV in storage works, but it ain't plugged in. It shows Saltine, Dishtowel, Tumbleweed, Toothpick, Hammer, Ringer, Mars, and shiny aliens called Gallions. They're all talking to this girl named Aria Vanir. Over."

"Vanir . . . Vanir," Dewey mumbled. He recognized the name as a leader in one of the SEALs' top covert squads. "Copy that, Headrock. I'll be right there. Over."

The lieutenant arrived in time to watch the Gallion healers mend the SEALs' injuries. He immediately contacted his commander. News quickly spread to Vice Admiral Jennings. By the time Jennings got there, Elizabeth was requesting permission for direct communication with the aliens.

Although Elizabeth was the squad's communications specialist, Jennings wondered why William wasn't leading dialogue with the aliens. He watched the scene closely to assess threats.

"Lieutenant, contact General Goforth," Jennings ordered. "Priority alpha alert."

From the viewing room of the royal suite, Arcthena cried out, "Your Majesty, come quickly! Word of the media rectangle is spreading."

"Let's see, let's see," the queen said as she dashed from her personal quarters to the viewing room.

"It's working, Your Majesty," Arcthena explained when the queen arrived. She quickly bowed and added, "Several American naval officials are watching their media rectangle, and they've called for Goforth."

"Splendid!" the queen responded as she sat in the largest chair and watched the hologram above the manifest machine in the center of the room. It showed Marshall, Dewey, Jennings, and the other officers intently staring at the plasma TV.

"Aria knows one of the SEALs as Miss Elizabeth. Your Majesty, I believe the Elizabeth SEAL recognizes us as friends now."

"Quite splendid! Call LeSom in here as well. And turn up the volume."

So now the queen and Arcthena watched the military officers as they watched Aria watching the SEALs and Gallions.

In the Healing Quadrant, Elizabeth motioned for Aria to stand behind her as she slowly approached the Gallions. She used the footprints that had just been made as a guide to stop before hitting the shield. Elizabeth took a deep breath and faced Ora. Her heart pounded, even though she was accustomed to speaking with potential hostiles.

Aria remembered how frightened she was when she first met Princess LeSom. She wanted to ease the tension between Elizabeth and Ora.

"Miss Elizabeth, they like the peace sign thingy," Aria explained as she raised two fingers in the air and wiggled them.

Elizabeth winked at Aria and confidently replied, "I got this one." The she turned to Ora, puffed out her chest, and raised her head.

"I am Lieutenant Elizabeth Manger of the United States Navy." Elizabeth cautiously raised her right hand in the air and made a peace sign. "To all the Gallions, I offer you peace. To those who cared for us," Elizabeth turned to the healers and continued, "I offer you my deepest gratitude."

Ora lowered the shield, extended two tentacle tips, and touched Elizabeth's fingertips. Elizabeth turned her hand to the side and gently shook Ora's tentacle, which felt more like seaweed than flesh.

"May we enjoy lasting friendship between our worlds," Ora offered. The SEAL and Gallion gently embraced.

Aria felt overjoyed. She threw her hands in the air and jumped around as though her sister had just won a softball tournament. The other SEALs in the Healing Quadrant slowly approached Elizabeth. They, too, made peace signs and shook hands-to-tentacles with the Gallions.

The queen, LeSom, and Arcthena cheered and celebrated for an hour. They had risked so much and had worked so hard for this moment of genuine acceptance. Witnessing the birth of friendship between humans and Gallions was worth the struggle—definitely.

Meanwhile in the storage and disposal center, Vice Admiral Jennings briefed General Goforth on Elizabeth's offer of peace to the aliens. They debated what to do next, since Elizabeth wasn't following standard alien contact protocol.

"Lieutenant, move this TV to the War Plans Room," Jennings ordered. "And hook up something to record what's happening for the Joint Special Operations Command. We'll need solid evidence to show the Pentagon. Remember, this is highly classified. It's a matter of national security."

Jennings turned to General Goforth and motioned with his head for the general to follow him. The two officers walked into a secure room.

"I think Bull's-Eye has been compromised," Jennings admitted. "I'll tell Ops to monitor movement of all the SEALs. Their trackers stopped working over an hour ago, so these recordings are all the evidence we have for proof of life. Wherever they are."

Goforth nodded, "Understood. I'll instruct my officers to assist. Let's brief hourly. Saltine has secured initial contact, but I still don't trust the aliens' motives."

"Another thing, General. The little girl, sir, she's Bull's-Eye's daughter."

Goforth looked Jennings square in the eyes and stated, "Then we've got a problem."

Chapter 22
William's Prison

William Vanir sat on the edge of a dirty mattress and listened to water drip from a battered sink just a few feet away. Drip . . . drip . . . drip. The irritating sounds reminded him of a Middle East prison cell where he had stayed three miserable nights before a SEAL team had rescued him. The cold, hard floor under his bare feet and the cinderblock wall behind him looked just like a North Korean compound where he had been forced to live for a week after being captured behind enemy lines. The severe pain in his leg and blood on his uniform were similar to injuries he had endured during a mission in South America. The stink of sewer took him back to other times that he had been held against his will and tortured severely.

William had always been proud of the fact that he never disclosed government secrets, no matter how much pain he had endured. He had thought about Lindsay and his daughters to survive his captors' cruel treatments and horrible prisons.

The door of William's cell opened. Ora entered, alone.

"Where have you taken my squad?" William demanded. He tried to stand, but the pain in his right leg caused him to hobble at best.

"Please relax, Captain Vanir. The other Americans have been healed and are recovering nicely. Let us help you."

William huffed and limped closer to Ora. Despite his pain, he wanted to appear strong and bold.

"Take me to them—now."

Ora gently explained, "First you must allow us to complete the healing process. You've lost much blood from your wounds."

"Your tentacles aren't touching a hair on my body," William snarled.

"Our healing methods are quite different from your culture's medicines and surgeries. We recognize your strong connections between the spiritual, mental, emotional, and physical bodies. We work on all of them to help your soul heal the wounds. I assure you, Captain Vanir, we mean the greatest good for you."

"Then why am I being held in this stinky, dirty prison?"

"This is where you've chosen to be," Ora calmly stated. "You deny yourself the healing we offer. Besides, you are not ready to forgive your captors."

"Like you?"

"No, like the ones who had locked you in prisons similar to this one. Doesn't it look familiar?" Even though William knew Ora had spoken the truth, he remained silent. "You created this surrounding during your healing process, when we were attempting to help you release wounds of hatred in your spiritual and emotional bodies. You instantly stopped us and built this barrier."

William rolled his eyes to the dingy, leaky ceiling. He thought the alien was full of it.

"I don't believe a word you're saying," William replied. "Your brainwashing techniques won't work on me."

"Most unfortunate," Ora responded. "You will live in your prison until such time as you learn this: Forgiveness gives. Especially when you learn to forgive yourself."

William remembered all the pain he had suffered on enemy lands trying to protect his wife and country. He vowed to make them pay for what they had done to him. William recalled the promise he had made to himself at Jeremy Hale's funeral—to die fighting for others instead of accepting forgiveness from Jeremy's mother.

"Save your forgiveness for sissies and preachers," William snapped. Now he used his fear and anger to give him strength. His body tightened. Adrenaline pumped through his veins. He was ready for combat again. This was the way William had learned to survive.

"Perhaps you can follow the lead of the other SEALs," Ora offered. "They, too, have suffered. But they allowed the process of healing and forgiveness to take place in their bodies. Their souls—"

"Enough!" William screamed. He couldn't tolerate hearing another word about forgiveness, healing, and his soul. These were ideas of weakness. Giving into them would prevent him from being strong and fighting with great courage. William flung himself toward Ora with the intention of choking her. Or at least pulling out her whiskers.

William hit a protective shield that Ora had placed around her body before opening the door to his cell. He moaned, grabbed his injured head, and fell to his knees. He gently wiggled his fingers to check for broken bones. He didn't feel any, but his wrists were sore from the harsh impact.

"Our healers can help you with that bump on your forehead and the bruising in your hands, if you let them. Remember, these shields aren't meant for sissies . . . or preachers. I advise you not to attempt a hostile move on me again, Captain Vanir."

Then Ora stretched one of her tentacles to the sink and touched the dripping water. Each drop turned into an ice cube until the sink was full. She tapped the end of the mattress. A white towel, clean bandages, and a heavy blanket materialized.

"I suggest you accept these gifts as a start of the healing process, William. Only your hate can make them disappear or turn them into something you despise."

With that, Ora left the cell.

Chapter 23
Lindsay's Dragon

Three days after the Gallions had beamed Aria onto their superspaceship, Jackie and Tommy rummaged through Aria's bedroom. They wore white plastic gloves as they frantically searched for the key that could unlock the mystery of her location. After looking on the teacups on her Hospitality Station, the handle of her hairbrush, and every doorknob, they finally uncovered what they needed on the top of Aria's alarm clock. A single fingerprint.

Jackie quickly opened the Crime Scene Investigator's Starter Kit that she had bought with her Christmas gift money. She and Tommy used the kit to lift Aria's fingerprint and press it on the tScan of Aria's tDiary. It worked. Jackie and Tommy had gained access to Aria's tDiary.

Next the tDiary asked for the password. They tried their names, their parents' names, their friends' names, Lindsay's maiden name, birth dates, call signs, sci-fi characters—anything Aria might use as a password. Nothing worked.

Jackie felt so frustrated. She had come so close to finding her sister and was blocked by an annoying password.

"Nuke it, Peanut!" Jackie yelled. She slammed her fist on Aria's desk and threw the dusting brush from the kit against Aria's closet door.

Tommy got out of Jackie's way while she threw her temper tantrum. He definitely understood why guys were more interested in having Jackie on their softball teams than asking her on a date.

Then Tommy timidly asked, "Peanut?"

"Yeah, it's my call sign for Aria. She hates it, but—"

Tommy rushed to the tDiary and typed p-e-a-n-u-t in the space for the password. It worked. Jackie and Tommy read Mitushi's message to Aria about being beamed aboard the *Rama* at one o'clock on June 20.

Jackie slowly stated, "That would be after Aria left Meredith's house—"

"Dude," Tommy nervously interrupted. "They swiped Aria."

In the royal suite of the *Rama*, Arcthena alerted the queen and LeSom about the communication leak of Aria's tDiary. The three of them watched Jackie and Tommy on the large-screen hologram above the manifest machine in the viewing room.

The queen anxiously tapped a light-blue crystal in her right tentacle and blared, "Mitushi, come to my viewing room at once. And ask your security crew to monitor holograms of the American military and the Healing Quadrant. We have a critical situation at Aria's home."

Mitushi teleported from the Navigation Chamber to the queen's viewing room and discovered what had happened. He and the queen debated the best option to contain this communication leak.

"I have to tell Mom," Jackie said.

"Dude, like Madam Southern Charm is going to believe her daughter has been taken by aliens. She'll think you've gone nuclear. Duh!"

Jackie argued, "Not if we show her this," as she pointed to Aria's tDiary.

Tommy shook his head and countered, "Dude, she'll think we made it all up. She'll go nuclear!"

"I have to try," Jackie said as she scooped the tDiary in her arms and ran through the house to find her mother. Tommy followed after her as best he could. Jackie finally found her mother in the backyard tending to her rosebushes and flowers. Lindsay often worked in her garden when she felt upset.

"Mom, Mom!" Jackie yelled as she jumped off the porch and ran across the yard, still clutching Aria's tDiary. Tommy was right behind her.

"My goodness, Jacqueline, what's all the excitement?"

Jackie quickly blurted, "Aliens took Aria. It's all in this tDiary. These Gallions have Aria in their superspaceship and—"

White lights with gold specks surrounded Jackie and Tommy. The yard, sky, house—everything—disappeared instantly. Their bodies locked in place so they couldn't even flinch. Next, a strong force, like an astro hurricane, picked them up and propelled them faster than imaginable. Five seconds later they gently landed in soft, cream-colored sand beside a waterfall.

Tommy looked around the tropical paradise and then said, "Dude, this don't look like the 'hood."

"Duh!"

Back at the Vanir home, Lindsay frantically called for her girls and Tommy. She ran around the yard and through the entire house three times.

Then Lindsay distinctly remembered Jacqueline's words, "It's all in this tDiary. These Gallions have Aria in their superspaceship and—"

So Lindsay went back to Aria's bedroom and stared at her desk. No tDiary.

Lindsay gasped and put her hand to her pounding heart. Maybe Jacqueline was right—aliens had Aria. She wondered if they wanted to study her psychic daughter. Perform experiments on her. Did these same aliens abduct Jacqueline and Tommy?

Now more than ever, Lindsay needed William. He always knew what to do, from getting Jacqueline to do her homework to protecting the family during hurricanes. However William wasn't there to help her. Lindsay was completely alone.

Lindsay slowly lowered her hand. All her life, she had fled from danger and controversy. She had been taught to be the good girl. Stay out of fights. Be seen, not heard. Obey. She realized that none of this would get her family back. She had to act.

Then Lindsay stood erect as she felt an unusual power insider her grow with each breath. The love for her family pushed aside her fears and self-doubt. She felt absolutely determined to do whatever it took to get her husband and daughters back home. But how?

At that moment, Lindsay remembered meeting Vice Admiral Albert Jennings at social events on the naval air station. Since he was the ranking official, he must know something about her husband and daughters. Without a second thought, Lindsay hastily drove to his office.

Since Lindsay had a military family pass, she was cleared through the outer gate. But she didn't have necessary identification to go inside the SEAL compound where Jennings worked. She had dropped William off at this spot hundreds of times and often wondered what was behind the tall fence and heavily guarded gate.

"Mrs. Vanir, you can't go pass this point," the guard firmly explained. "Please turn around."

"But I must talk to Albert Jennings about my daughters," Lindsay pleaded. She decided to tell a little white lie because the truth could get her admitted to a mental hospital. "Terrorists have taken my daughters and said they are going to kill William. I must see the vice admiral!"

Lindsay continued to argue with the security guard until he went side a booth to make a phone call. For a second, no one was around Lindsay or in front of her car. Only a long piece of wood in front of her bumper separated her from information about her family. Lindsay stomped the gas pedal and crashed through the inner gate. An alarm sounded. Military police chased her in jeeps to the building. Lindsay beat them inside.

"Albert Jennings!" Lindsay screamed as she ran down the hallway. She remembered, from a Family Day tour she had taken, that his office was on the third floor. The military police closed in on Lindsay. She ducked into the closest stairwell and sprinted to the third floor.

Someone announced on a loud speaker, "Invader alert. This is not a drill. I repeat. Invader alert. This is not a drill."

Alarms sounded inside the building. People panicked. Attack dogs barked. Military police grabbed their guns and scattered to their designated posts.

Lindsay flung open the third-floor door. She continued to yell for Jennings as she ran down the hall to his office. When she was only three doors away, two MPs grabbed Lindsay by her arms and ordered her to stand down.

"Albert Jennings," Lindsay screamed above the noise and chaos. "I need to—"

One of the MPs put his hand over Lindsay's mouth. The second one tried to put handcuffs on her. Lindsay struggled against their strength and quick moves.

Then something inside Lindsay stirred like a caged animal wanting freedom more desperately than life. That powerful, newfound part of Lindsay took over her physical body. A dragon emerged from within Lindsay, a dragon ready for the fight of her life.

Lindsay used her free hand to punch the first MP in the no-no zone below his belt. He cringed and bent over, at which time Lindsay thrust her elbow in the side of his head. As the second MP fumbled with the handcuffs, Lindsay jabbed her fist and a sharp edge of the handcuffs into his jaw. The blow forced him to turn his back to Lindsay, and she solidly kicked him in the seat of his pants. He fell and slid on the slick floor.

Lindsay swiftly escaped from the two MPs and dashed into Jennings' office. She shut the door behind her and locked it. To Lindsay's disappointment, he wasn't at his desk.

Jennings had been in a secure briefing room watching Aria meet the other SEALs and tell them about the Gallions. A lieutenant had alerted him about Mrs. Vanir's efforts to find him. Jennings hurriedly went to his office, surrounded by MPs.

The two MPs who had restrained Lindsay reached Jennings's door at the same time he arrived from the briefing room. The MPs had their guns drawn and were ready to attack the invader, who they believed to be a spy.

"Stand down, men," Jennings ordered. "She's the wife of one of our SEALs. I'll handle this—alone. And tell security I said the threat has been managed. Call off the dogs."

Jennings unlocked the door, stormed into his office, and yelled, "Mrs. Vanir, what the blazing heck are you doin'? You could have been shot. Do you have any idea—"

"The Gallions have Aria, my little girl," Lindsay interrupted in a hysterical tone. "She's only twelve!"

Jennings froze. His mind flooded with possibilities of how Mrs. Vanir could have found out about Aria and the aliens.

Lindsay calmed down a bit and explained, "Just an hour ago Jacqueline, my older daughter, and Tommy, Elizabeth's Manger's son, vanished in front of me. They were telling me that Aria was with the Gallions in a superspaceship. Then white lights surrounded them and—poof—they were gone. Sir, who are these Gallions? Why have they taken my children? Does this have anything to do with William's mission? You must help me!"

Jennings cautioned, "If I'm going to help you, Mrs. Vanir, we need your cooperation and vow of silence. Otherwise, I have to turn you over to the MPs. You won't like where they'll take you."

"Cooperation and silence," Lindsay quickly replied. "Yes, sir." She started to feel hopeful about finding her girls.

Jennings searched through this desk until he found a folder marked *Confidentiality Forms*. He pulled out five forms and told Lindsay she had to sign them before they discussed anything else. Lindsay quickly flipped to the last page of each document and signed her name.

"Remember, Mrs. Vanir. Confidential and top secret. I'll see to it that William is demoted and your family is torn apart if you breathe one word of this to anyone. You'll have to stay in a restricted area until the crisis is resolved."

Lindsay swiftly nodded her head. She understood the stakes.

"The Gallions aren't dangerous as far as we know," Jennings explained. "But we haven't confirmed William's location—yet. I'll take you to the War Plans Room where we are monitoring the Gallions' activities. An old TV is worth a thousand words."

Chapter 24
Seaweed and Chocolate

Jackie motioned for Tommy to hide behind a black stone with her and keep quiet until they figured out where they were. They kept their hands on their foreheads as much as possible to hide their eyes from what they assumed was a high-noon sun. They heard noises—human voices and laughing—from the other side of a coconut tree grove. Jackie tightly clutched Aria's tDiary under her left arm. She didn't want its vital intel to fall into the wrong hands.

"Follow me," Jackie ordered. "Keep low and don't say a word."

"No way, Dude. This is all your fault. You are so astro bossy. Nuke you—I wanna play in the waterfall." Tommy headed to the lagoon lined with black rocks.

Jackie grabbed him by the arm and warned, "You'll do what I say to keep alive, sailor. Besides, my dad outranks your mom. That means I outrank you."

Tommy wasn't impressed. He jerked his arm away from Jackie and took two steps closer to the water.

Jackie paused for a moment and then said, "Bet those waters are full of piranhas." Tommy froze in his tracks. He remembered movie scenes in which people had fallen into rivers and were eaten alive by fish. "They like little boys, Shrimp Bait. Bet they haven't eaten in days."

Tommy ran toward Jackie and said, "Alright, alright, I'll go. Just don't fall into any quicksand."

"Requesting radio silence," Jackie whispered as she squatted low to the ground.

"Dude, radios are so retro!"

Jackie huffed and demanded, "Just keep low and shut up." Tommy nodded his head in compliance.

Jackie and Tommy cautiously crept down the sandy path toward the voices. They made no noise, other than the squeak-squeak of the fine sand beneath their sandals. The path soon opened up to a wide beach, where Jackie and Tommy hid behind a large tree.

Jackie glanced around the tree and said, "Seven civvies at two o'clock. Three are cooking fish around a campfire. The others are—OMG—talking to tall golden dudes with punk hair at a picnic shelter."

"Let me see, let me see!" Tommy demanded. He stood and peered around the other side of the tree. "Holy guacamole!" Tommy yelled when saw the aliens. "Those must be the Gallions. They look almost just like that . . . that queen person who popped out of Aria's tDiary. Maybe they beamed us aboard just like they did Aria! Maybe—"

"Hush!" Jackie interrupted. "You'll compromise our location. We need more intel. Stay here, Tommy. I'm going in for a closer look. When I give you the signal, meet me at that large rock twenty feet to the right."

"What's the signal?" Tommy whispered.

"I'll whistle like I do when your mother thinks you've gone too far into the ocean." Tommy rolled his eyes and nodded.

Jackie dashed to a tree that was ten feet closer to the humans and aliens. After checking for any enemies around her, Jackie ran past the rendezvous rock and disappeared behind a group of berry bushes.

Tommy's heart pounded as he leaned his back against the tree and sat in the sand. He always wondered what it would be like to meet ETs. Now his hands trembled as he realized they were so close. Two minutes passed, but to Tommy it felt like an eternity.

Elizabeth squeezed between two berry bushes with an armload of coconuts and walked onto the beach.

"Hey y'all, we have more dessert! Tumbleweed, I need that sharp rock to open these."

Tommy thought he heard his mother's voice. He quickly jumped to his feet and looked in the direction of her voice. Through squinted eyes he watched a woman in a flowery dress hand two coconuts to another SEAL. Her hairstyle, her muscular back, and the poison frog tattoo on her shoulder told him one thing—it was his mom! Tommy felt so excited that he forgot Jackie's order and ran to his mother instead.

"Mom, Mom!" Tommy yelled as he approached Elizabeth. "Mom, is it really you?"

Nuke that kid, Jackie angrily thought to herself. *Tommy doesn't understand she could be an imposter. And he didn't wait for my signal.*

Elizabeth dropped the other coconuts in time for Tommy to jump into her arms. She swung him around and around, like they were playing spin-the-kid in their yard. She kissed him on both cheeks and gave him a big hug. Tommy usually felt embarrassed by public displays of affection from his mother. Today, however, he welcomed them.

"Jackie Vanir came with me," Tommy openly announced. He squirmed to free an arm and pointed to the last place he had seen Jackie. "She's hiding over there, somewhere."

Jean Neff Guthrie

With clenched teeth, Jackie snarled, "I told him to wait for my signal." Jackie quickly dug a hole for Aria's tDiary and piled rocks around it. She didn't trust anyone with Aria's secrets. Now for a weapon. Jackie backtracked until she found a long stick strong enough to serve as a bo. Jackie ran onto the beach with one goal in mind: Protect Tommy from the impersonator.

Jackie stopped within a few feet of Elizabeth and stood in an attack form, ready for a karate fight. Hammer—an African American with great strength and speed—quickly grabbed another long stick. He ran to Elizabeth's side, ready to guard his swim buddy.

"Put the stick down, Miss," Hammer politely urged. He tried to position himself between Jackie and Elizabeth, but Jackie wasn't going to let Tommy out of her site. And she certainly wasn't going to relinquish her bo. Hammer closed in on Jackie and sternly stated, "Put down the stick!"

Elizabeth shook her head and said, "Y'all, this is ridiculous. Put down the weapons before someone gets hurt." Neither Jackie nor Hammer so much as flinched. Elizabeth lowered Tommy to the sand and held his hand. She turned to Jackie and stated, "Jackie, these men and women are brave SEALs who train with and go on missions with your father. They all know Bull's-Eye." Then she turned to Hammer and said, "This is Jack—rather Jackie—Vanir, William's older daughter. The one who surfs, plays sports, and . . . obviously . . . fights."

"So you're Jack. I mean, Jackie. I always thought you were a boy, the way your father talks about you. I'm Luke Swan, but everybody calls me Hammer."

Hammer dropped his stick and extended his hand to Jackie, but she didn't trust him. She hit his hand with the end of her bo and started to circle around him.

"How do I know you're real?" Jackie demanded. "You probably tortured my father to get that information out of him."

"Jackie, you have to trust me," Elizabeth pleaded. "At some point in time, you put the armor down because there's no need to fight. We are who we say we are. Trust me."

"Oh yeah? Well, what does this mean?" Jackie gave a loud, shrill whistle. It was the signal she had wanted to give Tommy.

"It means Tommy swam too far into the ocean, and he needs to turn around before he gets caught in a riptide."

Now Jackie believed Elizabeth. Jackie relaxed, lowered one end of her weapon to the sand, and gave Elizabeth a high five.

"I just didn't recognize you in a dress," Jackie admitted to her.

Elizabeth explained, "The Gallions gave us these Hawaiian clothes when our wetsuits got . . . scratched up after being teleported."

"Teleported," Jackie repeated. "So the Gallions beamed y'all aboard as well?" Then Jackie briefed Elizabeth on Aria's disappearance, the messages in her tDiary, and being beamed from Virginia Beach.

Elizabeth quickly told Jackie they were in the Healing Quadrant of the *Rama*, a Gallion superspaceship. She said Aria had arrived on the *Rama* three days ago, and the Gallions had treated her like a princess. Jackie wanted more details about the mission, but Elizabeth explained the ormation was confidential. Jackie felt disappointed but understood the need for national security.

As Elizabeth was talking to Jackie, the other SEALs stopped what they were doing and gathered around the kids. Elizabeth introduced everyone and asked Jackie to brief the squad on how she and Tommy had ended up there.

One of the Gallions in the Healing Quadrant came up to the humans and announced, "Your midday feast is ready."

"Chow time!" Toothpick exclaimed. A lanky Native American, Toothpick had earned his call sign from his enormous consumption of food. As usual, he raced his teammates to be the first in line for lunch.

Elizabeth stayed with Tommy and Jackie to watch over them. Tommy glanced at Jackie for a signal as to their next move. Jackie just stared at the alien and swayed in unison with its whiskers.

The Gallion turned to Jackie and Tommy and said, "Greetings. It is an honor to meet you. I am Forkana, Hospitality Handmaiden for Queen Supreme Nashata."

Tommy's hand shook as he held up the Vulcan greeting sign from *Star Trek* and replied, "Live long and prosper!" He had practiced that dozens of times when he discovered the Gallions were for real.

Forkana held up two tentacles and replied, "Peace," as her whiskers parted into a U.

"Astro!" Tommy whispered. He smiled ear-to-ear. His dream of meeting a friendly alien had come true. For Tommy, this was more spectacular than all Christmas Days put together.

"This is Tommy, my youngest son. And this young lady is—"

"Jacqueline Vanir. Tenth grade graduate. No rank—yet."

Forkana tilted her head to Jackie and said, "Peace."

Tommy kicked Jackie to get her attention. He motioned for her to make the Vulcan sign as he had.

Jackie glared at Tommy as she sniped, "They're Gallions, not Vulcans! Duh!"

"They like it when you make the peace sign," Elizabeth explained to Jackie. Elizabeth raised two fingers in the air and said, "Peace, Forkana." She wanted to set a good impression for Tommy and Jackie.

"That's so retro," Jackie complained as she reluctantly raised her hand to offer the peace sign.

"Live long and prosper!" Tommy repeated with sparkles in his eyes.

Elizabeth chuckled as she said, "Let's go eat, kids. Help me pick up these coconuts along the way. We'll stack them at the end of the table."

When everyone had gathered around the table, Dishtowel gave a quick blessing. Forkana and her four apprentices lifted lids of five large platters they had placed in the center of the table.

The first platter contained fish the SEALs had caught by the waterfall and grilled on the beach. The second platter was full of cornbread the Gallions had made from their manifest machine. The third contained a bowl of blueberries and raspberries the SEALs had picked from the Healing Quadrant. Exotic cheeses, also produced by the manifest machines, lined the fourth platter. Piles of seaweed flowed over the edges of the seventh platter.

Tommy cringed when he saw the last platter and whined, "Seaweed? Do I have to eat that?"

"Absolutely," Elizabeth insisted. "I harvested it myself. Actually, this seaweed tastes like the wonderful salad Meredith's mother makes with ginger and olive oil."

"I think it tastes like spinach salad with raspberry vinaigrette," Dishtowel said. "Yum! Must be all the fruit in this place."

"Na, broccoli with almond slivers," Hammer countered. "Can't beat that as a veggie dish."

"Wheat grass blended with blueberries and protein powder," Mars insisted. "Great for bulking up."

Toothpick shook his head and said, "No, no—spring mix with walnuts and cranberries."

As the SEALs argued about the taste of the delicious seaweed, Forkana's whiskers parted into a U. Only she and her handmaidens knew the secrets of the mysterious seaweed. And they weren't telling anyone.

During the seaweed-tasting debate, Tommy complained to his mother about the bright lights. The Gallions had given sunglasses to the SEALs, so Elizabeth asked Forkana to manifest sunglasses for the kids. She took their orders—Maui Jim for Tommy and Oakley for Jackie—and asked one of her apprentices to create the sunglasses. The apprentice returned minutes later with the shades.

The Gallions had modified only Aria's sunglasses to transmit images to the U.S. Navy. The other pairs were delivered as originally ordered.

When the platters were empty, Elizabeth joyfully exclaimed, "Now for dessert!" She stepped lively to the stack of coconuts. Tumbleweed, a SEAL who had been a champion bull rider out West, gave Elizabeth a stone he had sharpened to a point.

"Ah, Mom, you know I hate coconut! Yuck!"

"Try it," urged Ringer, a female SEAL who had been a champion amateur boxer. "You'll like it." Then she winked at Tommy, which startled him.

"Listen to the women," Hammer suggested to Tommy. "They know about these things."

At that instant, Elizabeth cracked open a coconut and held it above her head. The inside was full of dark chocolate.

"When we manifested this room," Forkana explained to Tommy and Jackie, "we thought the coconuts on coconut trees were logically . . . nuts of cocoa."

"Like chocolate?" Jackie asked.

"Precisely. We offered to correct the trees, but Saltine and Ringer strongly insisted we leave them just as they are. Deformed."

"Deformed and delicious!" Elizabeth mumbled with half her mouth stuffed with dark chocolate.

"It seems to make the women very happy," Forkana admitted. "So we fooled Mother Nature. Ha, ha, ha."

The doors of the Healing Quadrant opened. Everyone stopped eating chocolate as Aria entered, followed by Princess LeSom and Ambassador Supreme Ora.

"Peanut!" Jackie yelled. She rushed to Aria and hugged her tightly, nearly tackling her to the sand.

Aria laughed as she embraced Jackie. Aria felt delighted to see someone her age, someone so close to her.

Jackie said, "I told you I'd protect you. We'll always stick together."

Aria smiled and responded, "When was I in danger?"

During these conversations, Jackie remembered she had buried Aria's tDiary. She uncovered it and brought it back to

Aria, but some of the ports and keys had been damaged by the fine sand. Aria started to cry.

Mitushi, who had joined the group ten minutes after LeSom and Ora had arrived, offered Peakte's expertise to fix Aria's tDiary. Aria liked what Peakte had done to her sunglasses, so she gladly gave her tDiary to Mitushi. She made him promise, though, not to read anything inside it.

Back at the War Plans Room in Virginia Beach, Lindsay watched her girls and Tommy interact with the SEALs and Gallions. She laughed as Jackie tried to fight Hammer and then cried when Aria entered the room.

Lindsay turned to the vice admiral and said, "Thank you for sharing this information with me. I just wish I were with my girls."

"You see, Mrs. Vanir, your daughters are safe," Jennings assured her. "We're monitoring them twenty-four by seven."

"So where is my husband?"

Chapter 25
Clean Sheets

Ora took a plate of food from where the SEALs had been eating to William Vanir's cell. When she entered, she felt delighted to see William resting on a larger mattress with white sheets and a fluffy pillow. The sink had stopped leaking, and the stench of raw sewage had disappeared.

"You've made improvements in your environment, Captain Vanir. Excellent."

William sat up in bed and replied, "Funny, they just showed up when I thought about how nice it would be to have a pillow and clean sheets."

"Funny about that," Ora agreed. "I see you fixed the sink and sewer line as well."

William just nodded again. He didn't want to admit to the alien that he didn't physically fix anything. He had no tools, not even duct tape. One minute William calmly thought about how nice it would be to enjoy silence and smell clean air. That second the sink stopped dripping, and the scent of tropical flowers filled his cell.

"Still, your walls remain around you."

William glared at Ora and replied, "I guess you're going to preach to me about forgiveness again."

"No, I brought you food. Your squad prepared the fish, berries, and seaweed. Our manifest machines made—"

William interrupted, "My squad?" He tried to stand, but the laser wounds in his right leg had gotten worse. So he sat on the edge of his bed and continued, "How are my teams? Are they still alive? Where are you holding them?"

"They are alive and well in our Healing Quadrant. All of them are in far, far better shape than you. Remember Captain Vanir, they allowed their healing to occur." Ora stretched her tentacles to present William with his midday meal. "They have eaten of this food and grow stronger. For your sake, I urge you to eat."

William sniffed the food first. He thought the seaweed smelled like Lindsay's homemade guacamole dip, which he enjoyed eating with chips while he watched football games. Although William always felt suspicious of foreign food, he was incredibly hungry and had a headache from low blood sugar. He took the plate from Ora and gobbled all the food in a matter of minutes.

"If you enjoyed that," Ora said as William returned the empty plate to her, "you should prepare yourself for our luau tonight."

"What?"

"In honor of our guests and the Earth's Summer Solstice, the Gallions are hosting a traditional luau this evening. As one of our guests, you are cordially invited to dine with us—Hawaiian style."

"Great! I'm ready to get out of here. Just take me back to my squad, and we'll go to your . . . luau."

"Will you agree to let our healers help you? More importantly, are you ready to forgive all those who have imprisoned you and brought you pain? Even yourself?"

William stared in silence at Ora. He now thought he could deal with alien tentacles on his body, especially if it meant alleviating the severe pain in his leg. The forgiveness part, though, still held him back.

"Most of your enemies are dead or in prison. Yet they hold so much power over you. Your rage toward them separates you from the One Power, from the Creator—the one you call God. These walls were constructed with your refusals to forgive or accept forgiveness." Ora pointed to the cinderblocks in front of William. "They, not the Gallions, prevent you from joining your squad and daughters."

"My daughters!" William exclaimed. He tried to stand but stumbled back to the bed instead. "What do you know about my daughters?"

"Aria called us to Earth, Captain Vanir, with her tDiary. She asked us to visit her family in Virginia Beach. Our queen felt quite impressed with the youngirl's intuition and capacity to see life on distant planets. The queen believed she could initiate friendly relations between our worlds through Aria. We've risked a diplomatic journey to Earth to make contact with your daughter."

William glared at Ora and replied, "Ever notice how your eyes turn purple when you lie? You know I don't believe a word you're saying."

Ora ignored him and continued, "Jackie discovered the transmissions between our queen and Aria. As a security precaution, we teleported her to the *Rama* as well. Being in the military, I'm sure you understand."

William shook his head and said, "Nothing you've said makes sense. You're nothing more than a slimy terrorist!"

Ora realized she needed to take a different approach. She thought humor might diffuse the confrontation.

"Have you and Albert Jennings heard Elvis from the stars lately?"

William raised his eyebrows. He remembered how Project Watchdog had detected Elvis lyrics before this mission had started.

Then Ora lowered her voice and sang, "You ain't nothin' but a hound dog, cryin' all the time."

William winced and covered his ears. He'd take a dripping sink over Ora's Elvis imitation any day.

"Princess LeSom makes it look so easy," Ora admitted. "But I think you get the message, Captain. We were the ones responsible for the transmissions to Virginia Beach."

William lifted his head and started straight into Ora's big, lavender eyes. He started to believe her.

"We teleported Aria, your aqualaports, and Jackie here. Our mission is one of peace and destiny. Please, let us help you."

William dropped his head and stared at the floor. He wanted to believe and receive healing, but he didn't know how to survive without his anger and resentment.

"Our healers are ready when you are, Captain. In the meantime, you might want to think about how nice it would be to have clean clothes, a place to bathe, and fresh bandages." Ora started to leave, but then she turned and said, "Just be a little bit—only a little bit—ready to forgive. We'll take care of the rest."

Chapter 26
The Luau

During that afternoon, Forkana and her apprentices worked with Mitushi's engineers to convert Holospace Three into a festive Hawaiian luau. They used records from the Gallery of the Worlds and the manifest machines to create the feast as authentically as possible. They tried to think of everything—old-fashioned huts, sandy beach, pigs and local seafood roasting over seven fire pits, evening sky with stars over the Pacific Ocean, long tables for over three hundred Gallions and Americans, and a stage. They even made grass skirts, leis, and seashell necklaces.

The hour for the luau arrived. Forkana, Arcthena, Peakte, PomPass, Marta, Gauzette, and Butch stood in two rows just inside the holospace door, ready to welcome the Americans and royal family. The other Gallions lined up behind them, still in two rows, to form a path from the entrance to the tables.

"They're here!" Forkana shouted. "Start the music."

A band of Gallions played traditional Polynesian music as the holospace doors opened. Mitushi escorted Aria Vanir into the luau, with a tentacle wrapped around her arm like a father walking his daughter down the aisle.

The Gallions cheered loudly when they saw their commander supreme and the youngirl. Aria wore a flowing muumuu with purple flowers, which she had asked LeSom to manifest for her. Aria had wanted a fancy dress to match her sunglasses.

The dimly lit holospace caused Aria's sunglasses to turn practically clear. She hardly noticed and didn't consider removing them. Aria enjoyed wearing her sunglasses so much that they had become a part of her.

Forkana cheerfully greeted them with a warm, "Aloha!" She placed seashell necklaces and leis around their necks.

Then LeSom entered with Jackie, who wore a Hawaiian shirt with the tails tied around her waist and cutoffs. LeSom had offered to manifest a dress for Jackie, but Jackie had told her to nuke the muumuu. No way was anyone going to get her into one of those overrated dresses.

As the Gallions cheered to welcome Jackie and LeSom, Forkana presented them with seashell necklaces and leis.

Next Ora escorted Tommy through the door. He blushed as the Gallions applauded in his honor. At his request, he wore a Hawaiian shirt with big lizards on it and green shorts to match. Forkana rubbed Tommy's cheeks with her whiskers as she gave him his necklace and lei. He turned beet red.

Dishtowel and Elizabeth entered the holospace next, followed by the other SEALs in order of rank. Forkana gave them necklaces and leis, and they followed the others to the tables.

The SEALs, as well as the kids, felt overwhelmed by the Gallions' generosity. The cheers. The gifts. The luau. Never before had they been treated with such grace and unconditional acceptance.

With such kindness from the aliens, the SEALs finally had believed the Gallions when repeatedly reassured that William was resting peacefully in another healing chamber. The Gallions had promised the SEALs that their leader would be ready for visitors in a few more days. Soon, the SEALs had stopped asking.

Once everyone was seated for the luau, Princess LeSom sang a traditional Hawaiian chant as a blessing. No one understood the words, but she explained it was an offering of thanks.

The feast lasted two hours. At the end of the meal, Mitushi rose from his place in the center of the front table and walked onto the stage. The music stopped, and everyone looked at the commander supreme.

"Welcome to our Summer Solstice Celebration, in honor of Earth and the humans we call . . . friends." The crowd cheered. Gallions banged their tentacles on the tables. The Americans clapped their hands.

Mitushi raised his tentacles to quiet the crowd. Then he continued.

"I have gifts for the Earth's children who are with us tonight. Aria, Jackie, and Tommy, please step forward." Everyone hooted and hollered again as the three kids shyly walked on stage and stood to the right of Mitushi. "The gifts, please." Three Gallions, each holding a crystal on a purple and gold pillow, marched onto the stage and stood on the other side of Mitushi. The crowd made ooh and aah sounds.

"As my crew knows, the original purpose of this mission was to introduce Queen Supreme Nashata to the youngirl, Aria Vanir, who invited us to visit her. Now we have two youngirls and a younguy on the *Rama*. The queen insists on taking precautions with any planets we explore and species we meet. As such, the three children will be offered challenges to master before they are permitted to meet our queen."

Mitushi turned to the children and softly said, "The challenges are not mandatory, but you will never know if you can pass them it until you try."

The kids stared at Mitushi with wide-open eyes, not saying a word. They felt nervous, but also excited at the thrill of an adventure.

Then Mitushi stood up straight and said, "Aria Vanir, do you accept our offer to master a challenge in order to meet our queen?"

Aria excitedly cried out, "Oh yes, yes, yes, yes, yes." Then she jumped in place and clapped her hands together. For Aria, this was a dream come true.

Everyone jumped to their feet and cheered for Aria.

Mitushi motioned for the first Gallion, who was holding a white crystal, to come closer. He grasped the crystal with his tentacle tips and held it in front of Aria.

"Aria, repeat after me," Mitushi instructed. "I accept this gift for my challenge."

"I accept this gift for my challenge."

"Now hold the crystal carefully," Mitushi said as he lowered the crystal to Aria's right hand. "Very carefully." Aria gently grasped the crystal. Mitushi quickly warned, "Hold tightly!"

Aria squeezed the crystal. It started to glow and buzz, just as the large white crystals of the manifest machine did when a Gallion requested something. Bright lights beamed from between Aria's fingers. Her skin heated from the crystal's rapid vibrations.

"Hang on for just another second or two," Mitushi encouraged Aria. He knew this part would feel awkward for her. He hoped she wouldn't go nuclear.

The crystal instantly expanded into a long sword of white light. Aria held its handle in front of her hip and surveyed every inch of the blade to the top, which towered above her head. It resembled a large, glowing feather with thousands of razor-sharp points. The sword looked like a cross between a light saber and the wing of a giant white dove.

"You have manifested the Gallion Sword of Purity for your challenge," Mitushi explained. "Light as a feather, isn't it?"

"Hardly weighs a thing," Aria replied as she swished the sword from side to side. Everyone on stage moved clear of the sword's edges.

"For you, its creator, the Sword of Purity holds only white light. That essence reverses to the energy of a black hole when anyone else touches it. No one else can lift your Sword of Purity, much less sling it around like you are doing."

"Nuke way," Aria sarcastically replied. She obviously didn't believe Mitushi.

Mitushi searched the tables for the largest and strongest SEAL, Hammer. He asked Hammer to join Aria on stage. The other SEALS hooted and hollered. Mitushi asked Aria to hand her sword to Hammer. When she did, the sword dropped to the stage and Hammer fell on top of it.

"Look at the sword now," Mitushi told everyone. "Once Hammer gets off it." Hammer released the sword, stood, and shrugged his shoulders.

Everyone stood and moved to get a good view of the sword, which had turned charcoal black. Hammer struggled again and again to lift it, but failed.

Mitushi explained, "Like your Earth legends of King Arthur, only the one connected to the Sword of Purity can reveal its light. Aria, it is time for you to take your sword."

Aria walked over to her sword and lifted it as though she were picking up a pen that had fallen to the floor. The sword buzzed as it filled with white light again. Everyone applauded Aria.

Mitushi motioned for Aria to stand on the other side of Tommy, and then he called Jackie forward.

"Jackie Vanir, do you accept our offer to master a challenge in order to meet our queen?"

Jackie stood up straight and firmly stated, "Affirmative, Commander!" Jackie didn't care that much about seeing the queen, but she never—ever—backed down from a challenge.

Mitushi asked the second Gallion, who was holding a green crystal, to step forward. He took the crystal and presented it to Jackie.

"Jackie, repeat after me. I accept this gift for my challenge."

"Sir, yes, sir. I accept this gift for my challenge. Sir!"

Elizabeth Manger giggled. She understood more than ever why Lindsay often commented that her Jacqueline was growing up to be just like William. The other SEALs wished all kids showed that much respect for authority figures.

"Remember, hold tightly," Mitushi whispered to Jackie as he handed the green crystal to her.

The crystal glowed and buzzed in Jackie's hand for three seconds, then it burst into a spinning discus. It reminded Jackie of the new, two-sided Frisbees her friends played with on the beach. Except Jackie's gift spun counterclockwise all by itself.

Mitushi delightedly remarked, "My, you have manifested the Gallion Roamer."

"Roamer?" Jackie questioned. "Doesn't look like it's going anywhere fast." Then she turned sideways and prepared to throw the roamer out into the crowd, just to see what would happen. All the Gallions ducked under the tables. The SEALs waved for Jackie to toss the roamer to them. They thought it was a game.

"Wait!" Mitushi pleaded. He swiftly grabbed the roamer and asked Jackie if he could demonstrate. Jackie agreed. The Gallions cautiously came out from under the tables and took their seats.

Mitushi tenderly balanced the Gallion Roamer on the tips of his right tentacle. His whiskers swayed as he thought about where he wanted to send the roamer. Without so much as a flinch from Mitushi, the roamer soared through the air and disappeared into the night sky. All eyes followed the roamer and strained to find it. Jackie wondered if Mitushi had lost her gift. Before she had a chance to interrogate him about the roamer, it flew back to Mitushi and landed on his tentacle tips.

"So it's a thought-controlled boomerang," Jackie assumed.

"More than that," Mitushi answered. "So much more. Look inside."

"How do I open it?" Jackie asked. She reached for the roamer to figure out how to twist it apart.

"Careful!" Mitushi warned. "Clasp your hands behind your back, youngirl." Jackie obeyed. "Now simply look into the center of the roamer, as though you are peering into a bowl of soup. Say, 'Show me your path.'"

Jackie looked into the top of the roamer and mumbled, "Show me your path." At this point she only halfheartedly believed Mitushi.

Scenes emerged of where the roamer had flown. To Jackie it was like watching the recording from a camera that had been attached to the roamer.

"Astro!" Jackie exclaimed as she watched pictures of the luau, dolphins jumping in a distant lagoon, lava flowing from a volcano, and colorful birds flying from tree to tree.

Tommy and Aria gathered around to watch as well. But they saw only the black top of the roamer. Mitushi explained the roamer could be viewed only by its creator, just as Aria was the only one who could lift her sword.

"I not only see the dolphins and volcano, but I understand what it's like to be them. When I watch the birds, I know I can fly like them."

"Tomorrow I will instruct you on the proper use of the roamer. For now," Mitushi gently placed the roamer in Jackie's palms, "just hold it very, very carefully."

Mitushi told Jackie to stand on the other side of Aria. He called forth Tommy.

"Tommy Manger, do you—"

"I accept your offer," Tommy hastily interrupted. "And I accept your gift. Thank you."

Elizabeth smiled. She felt so proud of her youngest son. He often had complained about not being able to hang out with his older brothers or play with their friends. She knew he'd be in the spotlight for years with the story of how he had accepted a challenge from the commander of an alien superspaceship.

Mitushi followed the same process to give Tommy a royal-blue crystal. When he held it tightly, it changed into a bow and arrows.

Carvings covered the wooden bow, similar to the symbols detected by Project Watchdog. The arrows glistened with white light, just like Aria's sword. They were contained in a brown leather pouch for Tommy to wear over his back.

Mitushi announced, "The Gallion Bow and Arrows!" The crowd cheered for Tommy.

"Astro!" Tommy exclaimed as he held the bow firmly in his hand and grabbed one of the arrows. He felt so excited, like a real-life Robin Hood on a new adventure. Tommy pulled back on the bowstring to try out his new gift, but Mitushi stopped him.

"I'll instruct you and the Vanir girls on how to use your gifts properly before you face your challenge. Meet me here in Holospace Three in the morning. We'll practice in an area that's a bit . . . less populated."

Peakte turned to Forkana and commented, "A new environment, here, by tomorrow morning? Mitushi has no idea how long it takes to drain the Pacific Ocean from a holospace."

Aria, Jackie, and Tommy thanked Mitushi and the Gallions for their gifts. Mitushi huddled the kids close to his side as they left the stage.

"Take care of your creations," Mitushi sternly urged, "as though your lives depended on them."

Princess LeSom romped to the middle of the stage and yelled, "What's a luau without the hula! Let's hula!"

Thirteen other Gallions came onto the stage and performed Hawaiian hula dances with LeSom. They shook their hips wildly as the band keep beat on native drums.

The hula dancers and musicians looked like they had been performing their whole lives. Actually, LeSom had downloaded accelerated programs of Hawaiian music and dance steps into their whiskers that afternoon. Gallions used over seventy percent of their brains to learn at phenomenal speeds.

That night the kids wanted to camp out in the Healing Quadrant with Elizabeth and the other SEALs. The Gallions quickly manifested hammocks for their beds and rock pillars to safely store their gifts.

"Miss Elizabeth, why is there an extra hammock?" Aria asked as Tommy's mother tucked her in for the night.

Elizabeth knew it probably was meant for William, so she ignored Aria's question. She and the other SEALs had agreed not to tell the girls about their missing father. They all expected him to join them at any time.

"Just . . . a mistake," Elizabeth answered.

Aria shook her head and argued, "Gallions don't make mistakes like that. Somebody's missing. Who's not here? I know . . . I just know someone is missing. Did you forget someone?"

"No one's forgotten, honey. SEALs take care of their teammates, you know that. Now get some sleep before your training."

Chapter 27
Starbucks

The morning after the luau, lights in the Healing Quadrant started to shine at the same time as the sun rose over Maui. Aria hopped out of her hammock and put on her sunglasses. Two SEALs—Ringer and Tumbleweed—were gathering berries and coconuts for breakfast. Aria started to help them when Forkana entered the Healing Quadrant with her hospitality apprentices. Her whiskers parted into a U as she prepared to announce a surprise.

"We have Starbucks this morning!" Forkana yelled so everyone would hear her. One by one the SEALs woke and walked to the picnic table where the apprentices had placed covered platters of food for breakfast. Elizabeth let Tommy and Jackie, who were both snoring, sleep a little longer.

When Aria and the SEALs settled at the picnic table, Forkana continued, "We've observed how Americans take part in a morning ritual called Starbucks."

"You mean, like, coffee?" Dishtowel asked.

"Precisely," Forkana answered.

All the SEALs clapped and cheered. They couldn't wait to get their hands on a latte, cappuccino, or espresso.

"So today we have stars," Forkana lifted the lid of one platter to show a mound of starfish. "And bucks." She lifted the lid of a second platter to reveal dozens of one-dollar bills.

The SEALs, all tremendously disappointed, stared silently at the platters. No one said anything. They didn't want to disgrace their hosts, who obviously didn't understand the true meaning of Starbucks.

Aria peeked between the SEALs' broad shoulders and said, "That doesn't look like the stuff Mommy gets. Where's the cup? Where's the machine that makes those swish-swirl noises?"

"Since we didn't know what you wanted," Forkana explained, "we decided to give you the stars and bucks to make your own." The SEALs gazed at Forkana with blank faces. "One of my apprentices will demonstrate."

Forkana nodded to a Gallion beside her, who picked up one starfish and a dollar bill in her tentacles. She rubbed them together for five seconds and then lifted them to her lips.

"Grande café mocha, light whip," the apprentice ordered to the star and buck. She opened her tentacles. The star and buck had transformed into a steaming cup of coffee. The apprentice took a sip. "Tasty, but a bit hot right now. I think I'll let it cool down for a minute."

Toothpick immediately grabbed a starfish and dollar bill. Everyone else watched as he rubbed them together and then spoke into his clasped hands.

"Special of the day with a shot of espresso, venti," Toothpick ordered. The next second he cried out, "Ouch, that is hot!" as he placed his cup of steaming coffee on the picnic table.

"Taste it, taste it," Dishtowel begged. He wanted to know whether it was good. Dishtowel despised the taste of bad coffee in his mouth. "And that's an order!" he joked.

Toothpick took a sip and replied, "Yum, delicious."

"Our special today is Kona coffee, grown in Hawaii. The manifest machine added a hint of cocoa as well."

"Got any cream or sugar?" Elizabeth asked as she grabbed a starfish and dollar bill. Another apprentice lifted the lid of a third platter to reveal a variety of creams, sugars, spices, and stirrers.

The SEALs fought over each other for the starfish and one-dollar bills. They placed their orders as Forkana's apprentice had demonstrated and enjoyed their morning Starbucks.

Aria pointed to the fourth covered platter and asked Forkana, "What's in there?"

"Oh, something fun for the tentacles—I mean tummies." Forkana lifted the lid to expose a pile of breakfast tarts and pastries. "All organic with no trans fats. And here," Forkana lifted the lid off the fifth platter, "we have eggs, shrimp grits, and sausage."

"Astro!" Aria exclaimed. She grabbed a coconut-shell bowl from the end of the table. "I love shrimp grits, especially the way Grandma Hiddleman makes them."

Forkana calmly replied, "Yes, we know."

Then Aria wiggled her index finger so Forkana would come closer to her face. Aria whispered into Forkana's whiskers that someone was missing. She wanted to know who and why.

Forkana whispered into Aria's ear, "Your Sword of Purity reveals all truths."

After breakfast the Gallions' first stylist brought fresh Hawaiian clothing for the SEALs. She gave high-performance athletic shorts and shirts to the kids because they were in training to face their challenge.

"I need more support in my sports bra," Jackie complained.

Tommy quickly joked, "Why bother with those buttons?" It was something he had heard his older brother say to be mean to a girl who liked him. Tommy didn't know exactly what it meant, but he thought it was funny as heck.

Tommy laughed so hard that he fell and rolled in the sand. He thoroughly enjoyed a moment of revenge for all the times Jackie had teased or tormented him. After enduring a minute of ridicule, Jackie picked up Tommy by his feet and shook him until he apologized.

Elizabeth, Ringer, and the Vanir girls bathed in the waterfall and changed into their clothes. Then the male SEALs and Tommy took their turn. While they were alone, the guys made up jokes about how long it takes four women to get ready in a waterfall.

Princess LeSom escorted the kids, who proudly carried their gifts by their sides, to Holospace Three. Ora had been invited to coach during the training, but she decided to spend the day with the SEALs. As ambassador supreme, she wanted to learn so much more about Earth's history and cultures.

"You must enter alone," LeSom said when she tapped a tentacle tip on the holospace door to open it. "May your gifts guide you to your truth."

Chapter 28
Aria's Training

Mitushi stood in Holospace Three, which was lined from floor to ceiling with glowing white crystals. He looked at his three Earth students who stood on the other side of the door with blank expressions on their faces. Mitushi sensed hesitation from their motionless bodies and felt compassion for them. He remembered how nervous and anxious he had been the day he had learned to use the gift his soul had forged from his crystal. Most Gallions spend months—years—learning to use the legendary arts of their ancestors. Now Mitushi had only hours to teach so much to the youngirls and younguy before their challenges. He wondered, how.

"The first lesson in your training is to step inside," Mitushi yelled across the holospace. "You won't learn anything in the corridor, I promise you."

Tommy, Jackie, and Aria slowly walked to Mitushi. They had expected to see practice targets or coaches to help them with their training. Certainly not plain columns of crystals.

Mitushi ordered the manifest machine to create Training Session 13: Beach Environment. Seconds later, tightly woven straw mats appeared behind the kids' feet. As they rolled out their mats and settled onto them, the floor turned into a beach like the one in the Healing Quadrant. On the other side of the holospace, gentle waves splashed on the surf.

"Negative ions are good for the brains," Mitushi commented. "Now, forget all you know about Earth's wars. Their purposes. Who fought whom. Their weapons. Forget everything." Mitushi paused. The sounds of waves on the beach started to mesmerize the kids. "Forget . . . everything."

The children started to sway and fought to keep their eyes open. Mitushi knew they would be more open to listening now.

"Think of your gifts as symbols. Long ago our Gallion ancestors instilled a sense of loyalty and duty by strengthening the soul and its destiny. We wondered why we were born. Why we chose certain paths. Why we met other species. We considered ourselves lost without understanding our purpose. Our ancestors turned to the legends of the warriors for clues. They proposed that the object of the Gallions' fight reflected an armor of discord inside each Gallion. As the fight is on the outside, so the fight is on the inside. Understand?"

Aria, Jackie, and Tommy listened to waves roll onto the surf. They looked at each other without saying a word. They each realized this wasn't the normal lesson of how to take down your opponent.

"The sword, roamer, and arrows show you the way to defeat your opponent by first ending the inner struggle that draws the conflict to you." For a few minutes, only the sounds of waves filled the holospace. Somehow the kids sat peacefully and quietly, not needing to ask questions or complain. They felt compelled just to listen.

Then Mitushi asked, "Aria, would you like to observe your sword again?"

Aria batted her eyes a couple of times and slowly stood. As she started to draw her sword, Mitushi reminded her to think of the sword as a symbol of her inner warrior.

Symbol of my inner warrior, Aria silently repeated in her head. *Symbol of my inner warrior.*

As soon as Aria's dainty fingers touched the handle, the sword popped out of the sheath. Aria clumsily tried to grab the sword, but it fell to the sand.

Mitushi exclaimed, "Excellent!" and clapped his tentacles. His whiskers parted into a U. He felt so proud of his student's accomplishment.

"But I dropped it," Aria whined. She blushed from embarrassment.

"Did you toss your sword on the ground?" Mitushi asked.

"No," Aria replied. "It just kinda fell there."

"You mean it flew there because it knew you wanted to draw it into the open."

"Oh?" Aria responded in an inquisitive tone. Something about Mitushi's statement made sense. To Aria, the sword felt like it had a mind of its own. Like it knew where it was supposed to go. In that moment, Aria got it. She carefully cleaned off the sword with the bottom of her shirt and put it back in the sheath.

Aria wiggled her fingers like a gunfighter in a duel. She imagined drawing her sword and holding it firmly above her head. Aria swiftly grasped the handle and hung on with all her might. The sword lifted itself over Aria's head, just as she had intended.

"It worked!" Aria yelled. She danced around with the sword above her head. "I did it!"

Mitushi continued, "Imagine a line from your heart to the tip of your sword." He helped Aria hold the sword straight in front of her as an illustration. "The blade is merely an extension of your arm, which is an extension of your heart.

Where your heart goes, so goes the sword. You don't have to force the sword up and down or right and left. Just feel it there. Now, Aria, try it—slowly at first."

Aria sensed the sword moving up to the right and then down to the left. It followed this path instantly, moving her arm to accommodate its new position.

"It's like the sword moves me instead of me moving it. Astro!"

"Now try cutting that piece of driftwood over there," Mitushi told Aria.

"What driftwood?" Aria asked. She didn't see any earlier.

"Over there," Mitushi pointed toward the surf, where a large chuck of driftwood had just appeared. The manifest machines had learned to create upon Mitushi's verbal intent, not just a direct command.

Aria marched to the driftwood with the confidence of a general. She felt the slice in the wood even before she raised her sword. In a flash, the sword hurled itself through the center of the log. Everything had happened so fast for Aria. She didn't even have time to think.

"Whoa, Peanut!" Jackie cried out. "You really nuked that log." She and Tommy ran to Aria for closer inspection.

Aria looked down and saw the driftwood in two clean pieces, as though a chainsaw had cut through it. For her, the movements had been effortless. She examined the blade. No scratches. No sawdust or sand. It had stayed in perfect condition.

Mitushi moved toward Aria and explained, "The sword not only moves with your heart; it answers your heart as well."

"You mean it talks?" Aria asked. She held the blade to hear ear but didn't hear anything.

"We'll save that for another lesson," Mitushi answered as he winked at Aria. A chill ran down Aria's spine, and she sensed a future adventure about her sword. "For now, let's focus on images. This bring us full circle to my original instruction. Aria, hold the flat part in front of you and look into it."

This time Aria complied with confidence, not doubt. She saw a brilliant reflection of herself, with white lights sparkling all around her face.

Mitushi inquired, "Aria, are you ready for your challenge from the Gallion queen?"

Chopping the log with great ease gave Aria the confidence to face any foe. She had faced quite an adventure so far to meet the Gallion queen. She wasn't about to stop now. Aria trusted Mitushi, her sword, and herself enough to accept the challenge.

Aria continued looking at herself as she affirmed, "Absolutely!"

Mitushi spoke slowly, "Ask your Sword of Purity to see your greatest enemy."

Chapter 29
Aria's Challenge

Chopping the log with great ease had given Aria the confidence to face any foe. She had overcome so many fears to meet the Gallion queen. She wasn't about to stop now. Aria trusted Mitushi, her sword, and herself enough to accept the challenge.

"Show me my greatest enemy," Aria commanded of her sword. She expected to see a gigantic dragon or man-eating dinosaur as her greatest enemy. Instead, she saw herself as a little girl, only three or four years old.

Little Aria, psychic and empathic, was seeing visions of her father as he had been tortured by his enemies. Aria had screamed and cried for hours. She had felt his agony and had wanted to do something to help him. She had reached out for him, but she couldn't touch him. She couldn't take him away or make the mean people stop hurting him. When Aria had tried to tell adults about what she had seen, they told her it was just her imagination. Eventually, Aria had dealt with this agony by ignoring and repressing her feelings. They existed deep in her subconscious until her sword revealed the truth and triggered a flood of emotional duress.

On the beach in the holospace, twelve-year-old Aria yelled, "Stop! Make them stop hurting Dad!" Then Aria threw a violent temper tantrum. All the anger bottled up inside her for years gushed out in seconds. Jackie and Tommy took eight steps back to avoid any backlash from Aria's nuclear outburst. They had never seen her go off the deep end like this. "Stop it!" Aria screamed at the top of her lungs.

"Your greatest enemy," Mitushi slowly stated between Aria's screams, "is not the foreigner torturing your father. It is the rage you repressed because you didn't know how to deal with these visions or your feelings at such a young age."

Aria turned to Mitushi and screamed, "What the hell are you talking about?"

Tommy gasped and muttered, "I can't believe she said the h-word."

Mitushi calmly explained, "You were quite empathic as a toddler and often felt what your father experienced when he went on missions. Unfortunately, no one knew how to help you deal with the horrors you sensed. You blocked them and eventually forgot about them, but they festered inside you. Now they are your greatest enemy. You must face them, consciously, and release them."

More tears ran down Aria's face as she yelled, "Release? Ag! Make it stop!"

"Keep screaming, Aria," Mitushi said, "Let it out. Release the anger. Give it . . . expression. If you can, ask your sword to show you how to release your anger."

Aria's body shook as she took a deep breath and shouted to her sword, "Show me how to release my anger!"

The holospace instantly changed from a beach to a barren field that once had been a thriving forest. Now, however, dead trees lay in heaps.

Aria quickly surveyed the mounds of dead trees. It looked like a deciduous graveyard. No leaves. No birds. Not even an acorn or sprout. Simply, desolate.

In a flash, Aria instinctively knew the outlet for her bottled-up rage. She screamed a shrill battle cry and then stormed through the dead trees with her sword. Slash, the sword chopped through two trees at once. Aria and her sword wasted no time in slicing through another three trees.

The intensity of Aria's emotions made her sword strike faster and harder. For Aria, chopping the wood was as easy as waving her arm in the air. She grunted like a professional tennis player serving a game-winning ace. Chop—ug! Often Aria visualized faces of the mean people in the trees before she struck them. Slash—ug! With each blow, an enraged part of Aria escaped from her body. Hack—ug! When Aria cut through the last limb of the final tree, her body went limp. She felt emotionally exhausted from the release of her anger. Aria fell to the ground beside her sword.

Jackie, Tommy, and Mitushi quickly came to Aria's side. They helped Aria stand and look at what she had accomplished. Acres of woodchips and mulch now fertilized the ground where the dead trees had been.

Mitushi announced, "Congratulations! You faced your greatest enemy, the conflict of repressed rage."

"I feel very tired," Aria admitted, "but relieved. Like I've taken off a backpack stuffed with dozens of books."

Mitushi continued, "One last part of your training, Aria, is a decision. Now that you've released your repressed rage, you have fertile soil upon which to grow a different emotion. A new way of feeling. What would you like to sow?"

Aria pondered for a moment, still dazed by the flow of emotions through her body. Mitushi suggested she ask her sword for guidance.

Aria picked up her sword and said, "Show me what to grow in place of my rage."

A scene appeared in the sword of Lindsay kissing newborn Aria on her cheek for the first time. Aria had completely forgotten that moment. Today, however, she remembered the unconditional love she had felt throughout her body with that first kiss from her mother. She wanted that feeling to stay and grow inside her more than anything else in the world.

In the midst of the woodchips, Aria touched her cheek where her mother had kissed her. The holospace changed again to a botanical garden full of huge red and pink rosebushes. Aria gazed across the acres of gorgeous flowers and manicured lawns in the holospace.

"Love," Aria softly said, "makes the whole world bloom."

Mitushi stretched his tentacle tips across Aria's shoulder, and they quietly admired the botanical garden she had created. Aria stepped closer to Mitushi and wrapped her arm around his back. He perceived what Aria had felt while watching Lindsay kiss her for the first time. Mitushi now understood the absolute best about humans.

Mitushi turned to Jackie and asked, "Are you ready?"

Chapter 30
Jackie's Training

Mitushi ordered the manifest machine to transform Holospace Three back into its original state—lined with white crystals. Jackie picked up her roamer, saluted Mitushi, and told him she was ready to face her greatest enemy now.

"Lesson number five," Mitushi slowly said as he took the roamer from Jackie, "patience comes with all great achievements. Listen and observe closely."

Jackie moved to Mitushi's side. She stared at him with wide-open eyes, eagerly awaiting his teachings.

"The secret to using the roamer is to first set your intention," Mitushi explained. "Simply glide your tentacle tips—in your case, hands—over the top of it and sense a desire to connect with something."

"You mean, like, connect with the enemy?"

Mitushi paused for a deep breath and then said, "Lesson number four again, back to basics." He asked the manifest machine for a white board and purple pen, which appeared to his side. He wrote:

I am apart from everything.

"This, Jackie, is the attitude of the loser. The one who thinks she must take something from someone else in order to win. You establish a foe within yourself even before you've engaged your roamer to search for something with which to connect. When you set your intention in this manner, you ask the roamer to find something for you to fight. A worthy opponent."

Then Mitushi wrote on the board, under the first sentence:

I am a part of everything.

"Which means what?" Jackie demanded.

"Which means you gather intel from a need to appreciate, not a need to fight."

"Oh," Jackie mumbled. She started to get it. "I like gathering intel."

"Generally, your military's purpose for gathering intel is to position itself for a more advantageous attack. Centuries ago, the Gallions used to think that same way. Our fighting nearly destroyed our planet and its nearby wormhole. Then my great-great-great-great grandmother decided, while she was queen, to learn something new about our opposing Gallion faction every day. Books and recorded information weren't enough. She really wanted to understand why we Gallions—with different markings down our backs—had so much hatred for each other. Her scientists created the first version of a Gallion Roamer. Antiquated, but it served its purpose."

"What purpose?" Jackie interrupted.

Mitushi answered, "The purpose of being fearless enough to connect fully with your enemy. You see, Jackie, the result of gaining knowledge about the enemy wasn't important after all. What changed the Gallions was the process of becoming fearless. When we—starting with our queen—no longer contained a foe within ourselves, we stopped wanting to fight. Our peace talks started to work. We began to resolve our differences without killing each other or destroying our lands. Slowly we unified as a collective land of Gallions under one queen supreme. Since then, our power has multiplied one hundredfold, and we've been honored with top positions on the Intergalactic Oversight Council."

Jackie joked, "Just by . . . tossing this roamer over a couple of borders?"

"Just by knowing we all have enough. When we are a part of everything, we have pure prosperity. We don't have to engage in battle or dominate another Gallion in order to gain something. We simply attract that which we want."

Jackie's eyes widened as she asked, "Is that how you make things appear and change in the blink of an eye?"

"Mostly. Having a manifest machine in a holospace gives us an advantage. Again, it has taken the Gallions centuries to master these prosperity concepts. I will teach you as much as I can, but be patient with yourself."

"Let's rock," Jackie urged. Patience was not her forte.

"Step forward and hold the base of your roamer with one hand," Mitushi instructed. Jackie followed his orders precisely. "Free your mind of any need to fight someone or resist anything. Feel a flow of energy from your heart to the roamer." Nothing happened, and Jackie became fidgety. "Remember patience," Mitushi told her. "Remember—"

The roamer began to spin counterclockwise. It flew vertically three inches and hovered over Jackie's hand.

At this point, Mitushi touched a tentacle to Jackie's shoulder and said, "Excellent! Remember to keep the flow from your heart to the roamer. Your gift runs on that powerful energy. Now set the intention for your roamer to guide you to the whole."

"Guide me into a hole? That doesn't make any sense."

Mitushi wrote the word *whole* on the whiteboard and then repeated, "Guide you to the whole. The wholeness. The connectedness. The—"

In a flash, the roamer flew out of sight. Jackie gasped. Tommy and Aria jumped to their feet and applauded.

"Congratulations!" Mitushi exclaimed and squeezed Jackie's shoulders. "You got the message to your roamer."

Jackie looked down and admitted, "I really didn't do anything."

"Perfect. The flow should be effortless. Painless. Easy. Especially since we upgraded the roamers with hypersensitivity and altability." Jackie looked confused. Mitushi consoled her by saying, "We'll cover that in future lessons." Then he patted her on the back and added, "Just stay alert."

"So where's my roamer?"

"Gathering intel, as you say. Since it's powered by the flow, it passes through objects without breaking them. It bends the rules of time and space to move from one dimension to another as easily as you walked from the corridor into this holospace. Astro, as you say."

Jackie pointed to the last word Mitushi had written on the whiteboard and asked, "So my roamer gathers intel on whatever I need to know to connect with my wholeness?" Mitushi nodded. "So I move from my foe into my flow, eh?"

"Masterful!" Mitushi cheered. You've learned—"

Aria interrupted, "The roamer is back. Look!"

The roamer flew to Jackie and hovered at eyelevel, spinning and buzzing so fast that it nearly made her dizzy. Mitushi lifted Jackie's arm, palm up. The roamer gently landed in her hand. "Connect," Mitushi softly urged Jackie as he lowered his tentacle, "and see."

Chapter 31
Jackie's Challenge

Jackie gazed into the top of the roamer as she had during the luau. This time the roamer showed her polar bears on icebergs, giant lizards in a desert, little frogs on a tropical island, and whales trying to escape hunters. Jackie not only saw the animals, but she instantly understood their dilemmas, desires, and feelings. She realized how humans had hunted these animals or destroyed their habitat until they were few in number and faced extinction.

Jackie sensed the pain and strife of these dying animals deep in her own body. The pointless killings angered her. Jackie's fingers tightened around the roamer.

"We must help them," Jackie pleaded to Mitushi, "before they all die!"

"Perhaps that is your greatest challenge. To learn to adapt on Earth so no other creature must perish."

"But I'm just a girl. Can't you do something with your superspaceship? Can't you nuke the ones who are killing them?"

"That is not my mission," Mitushi calmly replied. "Besides, nuking the hunters all at once destroys the balance. You must lead your people to find a better way to coexist on this planet so all life-forms prosper."

"But how?"

"So far your nature has been to seek, compete, and take. You've believed you must win a fight or possess a precious resource in order to feel prosperous. Your winnings make you happy temporarily, but later you aren't satisfied. You again seek to fight or take something else, believing that this new item will make you feel even more prosperous. For a moment you are happy, but then—"

Jackie interrupted, "Then we want to take something else. And it goes on and on."

"Precisely. This lifestyle causes humans to be apart from everything."

"So what's the better way?"

"Oneness. Total prosperity. It happens, Jackie, when you know yourself and everything else around you so well that you automatically feel blessed. Everything flows to you effortlessly. You have no need to dominate and control. Try the roamer again—and again. The more you consciously connect, the more insight you receive."

Jackie launched the roamer four more times. With each return trip she gained a new perspective from the lives gathered by the roamer. She felt sad when she sensed Chinese baby girls being born and then abandoned, innocent kids killed during drive-by shootings, and prisoners staring up at the walls that kept them captive. She didn't realize there was so much despair in the world. However, Jackie felt joy when she watched Native Americans teaching their children the dances of their ancestors, wild dolphins swimming beside a tour boat, and eagles feeding their young.

"Are you ready for your next challenge from the Gallion Queen?" Mitushi asked Jackie. "To face your most worthy opponent?"

Jackie shrugged her shoulders and confidently replied, "Yeah, I got this one." She assumed the opponent simply would appear in the roamer.

Mitushi's whiskers spread out as he counseled, "Be prepared."

The roamer began to spin and hover, just as it had before. This time it moved only ten feet away and transformed into a Japanese black-belt warrior.

The floor underneath Jackie and the warrior became a mat used during top karate competitions. A referee appeared between them.

Jackie turned to Mitushi and yelled, "Hey, this ain't fair. Look at how big he is. He's way older than me. He's—"

The warrior quickly approached Jackie with combination spins and hits. Jackie ran off the mat and started fussing at Mitushi, who crossed his tentacles and remained quiet. The referee gave Jackie a warning.

Jackie continued to plead with Mitushi to stop this unfair match. She had no idea how she possibly could stay alive, much less win.

Mitushi finally said, "You accepted this challenge. Now connect with your opponent. Don't let size and sight fool you. Right now your inner foe of fear has defeated you before you've made the first punch. Let it go. Focus on the flow. Connect with your—" Mitushi pointed to the whiteboard.

"Wholeness," Jackie said with a slight tremble in her voice.

"The purpose isn't hitting or kicking to win. The purpose is connecting to enjoy the oneness."

Jackie turned and walked back to the mat mumbling, "I so don't get what the commander says. But I like the way he says it."

Tommy and Aria chanted, "Jackie, Jackie, Jackie." The warrior and referee took their positions. Jackie stepped onto the mat. She had never backed down from a good challenge. She wasn't about to start now.

Connect with my opponent, Jackie said to herself. *Connect with my opponent.* She paused to clear her mind.

The warrior ran toward Jackie. She felt a flow of energy from her heart to his, just as she did when the roamer had started spinning. Somehow Jackie now sensed his thoughts and next moves as though time no longer was linear. She felt the warrior's movements in her heart before she saw them with her eyes.

As the warrior quickly advanced toward Jackie with a sliding side kick, she instinctively dodged it with ease. In her body, Jackie knew the warrior was going to follow with a middle punch to her stomach. She stepped to the side to avoid the hit. Jackie sensed the warrior was off balance on his left leg. She simply shifted her position to trip him and then pinned him to the mat.

The referee declared, "Match awarded to Vanir!"

Aria and Tommy cheered and gave each other high fives. Mitushi's whiskers turned U as he bowed his head in respect to his student.

Jackie felt stunned that she had pinned her strongest opponent with the least amount of effort. The accomplishment wasn't about winning, but about learning she had the ability to connect with anything—even the scariest opponent imaginable.

The referee helped the warrior to stand. Jackie and her opponent bowed to each other.

The warrior winked at Jackie, and then he transformed back into the roamer. Two seconds later, the roamer sucked up the mat and referee.

The roamer played back the match for Jackie. She watched herself change from scared girl to confident winner, simply by releasing her fears and connecting.

"You can watch that match whenever you wish," Mitushi said to Jackie. "More importantly, you can choose connection to wholeness over your fears at any moment. Remember this, and you can receive infinite blessings of prosperity.

Mitushi turned to Tommy and said, "Talking about the infinite, let's work on your archery lessons."

Chapter 32
Tommy's Turn

Tommy felt insecure as he walked with his bow and arrows to Mitushi's side for his lesson. The Vanir girls had faced immense challenges and passed. He certainly didn't want to be the only one to fail. Tommy always had wanted to be aboard an alien space craft and live new adventures each day. But right now a part of him just wanted to go home and build sandcastles.

"Let's start with the basics, Tommy, since we usually have to go back to them anyway." Tommy nodded. Mitushi noticed that the boy's body trembled slightly, so he stretched four tentacle tips across his shoulders to comfort him. "Repeat after me, Tommy. Altability"

"Altability, sir."

"Excellent. Do you know what that means?"

Tommy shook his head. His eyes widened and his heart pounded as though he was about to learn the greatest secret in the world.

"Then it is good that we start with the basics. Altability is the speed of infinity. It is seeing yourself all together in two places at once. In your case, it is seeing your arrow all together in two places at once." Mitushi stroked the white feathers on one of Tommy's arrows. "Let's give it a try."

Mitushi ordered the manifest machine to create a round target, which then appeared twenty-two yards away. Mitushi instructed Tommy on how to grip the handle of his bow, place the arrow on the rest, and draw back the string. Although the bow was almost as tall as Tommy, it felt light to him just as Aria's sword did to her. Mitushi gave Tommy a few pointers on aiming.

"Focus on your target, Tommy. Let the arrow find its own path there."

Tommy put the bow aside and complained, "That doesn't make any sense. Shouldn't I align the arrow with the bull's-eye and adjust for wind or something."

"You can stay stuck in that procedure," Mitushi responded. "Or you can move into altability. Tommy, this isn't any ordinary bow. These certainly aren't any ordinary arrows. Take a break to look into a feather of an arrow."

Tommy glanced at the end of an arrow and then shrugged his shoulders. He didn't get it.

So Mitushi demonstrated. He held the end of the arrow in front of his face and gazed into one of the feathers. Mitushi told Tommy to do exactly the same.

This time Tommy saw images of the target's center, the bull's-eye, in the white lights of the feather. He felt so excited! He jumped around and then ran over to Aria. He wanted to show the images to his friend. However, Aria saw only white lines and sparkles.

Mitushi explained that only Tommy could bend his bowstring and see the images in his arrow's feather. Only Aria could lift her sword and see answers in it. Only Jackie could observe images in her roamer.

"Now try shooting your arrow," Mitushi suggested. "Think about your arrow being in two places at once. Feel it between your fingers and then envision it being in the center of the target. Focus on both being true at the same time."

Tommy pulled back the bowstring and prepared to shoot. Unfortunately, he started to doubt himself. What if he failed? What if the arrow hit a crystal instead? What if he messed up so badly they kicked him off the superspaceship?

Black clouds of fear and insecurity covered the image of the bull's-eye in Tommy's mind. He shot the arrow, but it sailed off path and hit a wooden stand that supported the target.

Mitushi calmly stated, "Not bad for a first try."

Tommy turned his head and lowered his eyes. He felt humiliated.

"You know your target," Mitushi continued. "You just don't know yourself. Altability starts with you. Your connection to your arrow, bow, arm, heart, and your head. Hold another arrow in front of you to form a straight line from your eye to the point of the arrow."

Tommy followed Mitushi's instructions. Mitushi slid one of his tentacles from Tommy's shoulder down his arm to the arrow's tip.

"These arrows know what's in your heart," Mitushi whispered. "They sense whether you know where you are in life and where you want the arrow to go. The key is to start with yourself—with your inner connection. Without that, you might as well not even draw the bowstring."

"How do I know where I am in life? I can't even drive."

Mitushi replied, "You stand firm in the truth of what you believe. You courageously speak your truth when it needs to be told. You stand in your own light and not the shadows of others. Tommy, your connection within is the only thing that lasts forever. Know it, and you master infinity."

Mitushi gave Tommy time to ponder what he had explained. When Tommy started to nod his head, Mitushi knew it was time for the next step.

"Are you ready for your challenge from the Gallion Queen, Thomas Manger?"

"Yeah," Tommy quickly replied without thinking. "But . . . I . . . haven't even hit the outer circle of the target yet."

"Irrelevant," Mitushi insisted. He touched a blue crystal on his tentacle and said, "Marta, lock onto the younguy beside me and return him to his home—preferably near his family."

White lights surrounded Tommy. Aria and Jackie backed away from Mitushi and the beaming portal. In a flash, Tommy had disappeared.

Jackie and Aria demanded to know what had happened to their friend. Mitushi requested the holospace's manifest machine to view images of Tommy in his new environment.

Tommy landed in his backyard where his older brother, Drake, was playing tag football with his five closest friends. They stopped the game when they saw Tommy and asked him a dozen questions.

"Where have you been?"

"Don't you know how scared everyone's been?"

"Dude, what's with you?"

"Why did you run away?"

"Dude, what's with the bow and arrows?"

"Where did you get the astro threads?"

Tommy held up his hand and yelled, "Dudes, just chill! I'll tell you what happened when y'all shut up." The older boys stopped talking. Tommy took a deep breath for courage and blurted, "The Gallions—those aliens I tried to tell you about—beamed me aboard their superspaceship. Aria and Jackie Vanir are there as well. Mom, too, by the way."

Drake rolled his eyes and said, "Mom's on a mission, probably fighting some terrorist group. Don't lie about Mom, you little punk." Then he shoved Tommy.

"I'm telling the truth," Tommy persisted. "These are good aliens. They have Hawaii in a Healing Quadrant for Mom and the other SEALs. They gave us food and astro clothes like this." Tommy pointed to his sleeveless sports shirt with mesh siding. "Dudes, we even had a luau last night. That's when I got this gift." Tommy held up his bow and arrows with pride.

Drake grabbed the bow and an arrow from the leather pouch strapped to Tommy's back. He tried to draw the bowstring, but couldn't. Each of his friends attempted to shoot arrows with Tommy's bow. The bowstring refused to budge even a millimeter for any of them.

"It's broken," Drake concluded. "Worthless piece of crap."

Tommy stood up to his big brother and yelled, "Is not. It's my lesson, not yours. And the aliens are real. Aria was right. The Gallions are here!"

Tommy paused, mostly because his throat hurt from shouting. He stared up at the eyes of the older boys who completely encircled him. They all frowned and glared at him. Drake started laughing at Tommy. One by one, his buddies joined in the ridicule. They started slapping Tommy on the head and punching him on the shoulders.

In the past, Tommy would have felt humiliated and run to his room. Or he would have agreed with the older boys that it was all a hoax. Not today. Tommy sensed a fire in his heart and refused to die down from the shame. It blazed within him and gave him the courage to speak his truth.

"Dudes, the Gallions are our friends!" Tommy persisted. "They gave me this bow and told me that I was the only one who could pull back its string."

The older boys still didn't believe Tommy. When they got bored of tormenting him, they returned to their game of football. Tommy called out to his older brother, but Drake told him to get lost.

Tommy stood his ground and didn't run anywhere. Instead he held an arrow in the bow. He patiently waited until one of the boys, Patrick, dropped back for a pass. Tommy swiftly pulled back on the bowstring as he remembered Mitushi's teachings.

Focus on your target. Let the arrow find its own path there. Altability starts with you.

Patrick released the football, and Tommy's eyes followed it like an eagle diving for prey. Tommy released his arrow. It buzzed through the air. *Zing-zing-zing-zing-zing.* The arrow landed smack in the middle of the football. The football exploded, and the arrow returned to Tommy's feet.

While Tommy tossed the arrow into the pouch on his back, the older boys started to run at him. Oh, they were extramad.

Back on the *Rama*, Mitushi told Marta to beam the younguy back to Holospace Three. A shield of white light surrounded Tommy just as Drake tried to pounce on him. Tommy landed on the holospace floor with one foot in the air, ready to escape from the fuming older boys. As a result, he tumbled to his side. Mitushi stretched a tentacle to hoist Tommy back to his feet.

Mitushi sternly stated, "Lesson number six, choose your targets appropriately."

Tommy giggled and replied, "Yeah, but it felt so good."

"Congratulations anyway, Tommy. You passed your challenge."

Aria and Jackie clapped and chanted, "Tommy, Tommy, Tommy." Then Tommy raised his hand and shook his head to stop them.

"I'm not quite done with my challenge yet," Tommy explained. He walked to Aria and said, "I'm sorry I didn't believe you about the Gallions. I'm sorry I told you they weren't real and you were stupid and all that. My bad. I just told Drake and them that you were right. You know, they still didn't believe me."

Mitushi looked Tommy in his eyes and asked, "How did you feel when you pulled back your bowstring to shoot your arrow at the football?"

"Nervous at first, Commander Supreme. Then this astro wave of . . . of . . . okayness splashed over me. Like I was in the zone on my boogie board. Everything stopped except me, the bow and arrow, and the football. It was like the arrow wanted to hit the football, and all I had to do was let go."

"True, so true," Mitushi replied. "What did you sense in that moment?"

"That I was a part of everything, all together. Like I saw the whole puzzle of life as one big moment instead of a bunch of separate pieces. And that one moment was everything. You know?"

"You've experienced infinity," Mitushi explained. "Even if for only a brief moment. You'll carry that sense of being a part of the whole puzzle with you for the rest of your life. Whenever you need courage to face a difficult situation or life just doesn't seem right, simply gaze into a feather of your arrow. It will help you remember that moment of infinity."

In a perky tone Tommy replied, "Thanks, Commander Supreme." He ran his fingers across the feathers of an arrow, sensing again the infinity of the moment.

"Now for the finale," Mitushi announced. "Form a triangle in front of me." The kids quickly complied with Mitushi's order. "Touch your gifts together. Aria, the tip of your sword with the point of Tommy's arrow and the center of Jackie's roamer." White lights sparked where the three gifts united. "Hold steady, no matter what happens."

The white sparks expanded into a brilliant pillar of light. It stretched from the ceiling to the floor, and it grew as wide as the triangle that the kids had formed. The pillar resembled the columns in the holospace and corridors, only it wasn't made of crystals. Just light.

"What is it?" Jackie shouted over the buzzing noise from the white lights.

"The quality of life when love, prosperity, and infinity meet. A power so much greater than its individual parts." Mitushi paused and stretched his tentacle tips across the shoulders of his students. "Teach each other. Be there for each other. Meeting your challenges today brings you an awareness most never dream feasible."

Mitushi admired his pupils' progress with their first Gallion lessons, even though they were just humans. While he enjoyed the bliss from the pillar of light, Mitushi pondered how the other Vanir would tackle his deepest challenge.

Chapter 33
William's Dream

As Jackie, Aria, and Tommy completed their challenges, William sat on the edge of his bed and tapped SOS against the wall. Over and over and over. Doing something helped get his mind off his infected, painful leg and the fever that had started a few hours ago. William knew he didn't have much strength left. He decided to rest a while, hoping that the fever would break after a few hours of sleep.

Sound asleep, William dreamt he was on a camping trip. No SEALs or Gallions. No prison walls. William sat on a log by a fire roasting hotdogs and marshmallows under a clear night sky full of stars. He felt uncommonly relaxed and wanted this moment to last forever.

In William's dream, someone came out of the dense woods holding an unusually long flashlight. It was Aria. A wolf howled, and she ran to her father's campfire.

"Dad, we must leave," Aria pleaded. A limb cracked in the forest near them, and Aria worried that a bear was approaching. "This place isn't safe. Please, come with me!"

"I can't leave now," William explained. "I'm not done cooking my hotdog. And look at all these marshmallows we're going to roast. Yes, this will be a long night of camping. What fun!"

The wolf howled again, and Aria shivered. She again demanded they leave at once. William just revolved his stick to heat the other side of his hotdog.

Then Aria noticed a large cut on her father's right leg. It was still bleeding. "Dad, don't be dumb. You need medical attention."

"Nuke that!" William shouted at his daughter. "I'll stay here as long as I want!"

Something rustled in the bushes near their campsite and scared Aria. She again pleaded with her father to douse the fire and leave immediately.

"I don't know where else to go," William calmly answered. "I've been camping here for . . . a long time. So nice of you to join me!"

Aria jumped to her feet and looked around the campsite until she found a path of sand. It led into the darkness, but Aria heard running water in the distance. She assumed it was a river that they could follow to get out of the dangerous forest.

"Come on, Dad, let's go!" Aria pleaded as she pointed her flashlight to the sandy path. "It's our way out. We have to get help for you. Hurry!"

William turned his stick again and replied, "I'm content to stay right here.

"Follow me!" Aria exclaimed as she took three steps down the path. "I have to get you out of here and find a doctor."

"I don't need any healing," William insisted. "I'm fine just the way I am, right here at this campsite."

"Captain Vanir!" a friendly voice called from down the path. Tommy entered the campsite, carrying a fishing pole and tackle box.

William limped to Tommy and said, "Good to see ya, kid! Sit down and enjoy a hotdog. We've got plenty for everybody. You can use my stick when I'm done. It'll be just another minute or two."

Aria pointed to her father's bleeding leg and made a big-eyed look at Tommy. He got the message.

"You must leave now, Captain Vanir," Tommy insisted. "Your wound has made you very, very sick. You must let us help you."

"No thanks, Tommy. I'm great. Another marshmallow or two, and I'll feel as good as new."

Jackie, with a Frisbee in hand, ran down the sandy path to join Aria and Tommy. Aria quickly pulled her aside to explain their father's condition. Jackie, too, tried to convince her father to leave with them. He again refused.

Finally William stood and demanded, "Will y'all just take a seat round the campfire and eat hotdogs with me? There's plenty for everyone. And that's an order!" He waved his arm to motion his daughters and Tommy to join him. Then William stumbled from the pain in his leg.

Aria and Jackie helped their father back onto the log where he had been sitting. They insisted he go with them to get medical attention. Again, he angrily refused.

"Why do you want to stay in this darkness instead of following us?" Aria asked.

William shook his head and softly replied, "I'm not sure. I don't really know. I've been here so long I don't know what else to do."

"Come with us, Father," Jackie pleaded. "Follow Aria's flashlight down this path."

William looked into his daughters' eyes. He wondered, for the first time in a very long while, why he had been camping in the wilderness. Perhaps his girls were right. It was time to go home.

Jackie and Tommy supported William so he could walk without putting much pressure on his right leg. They followed Aria down the sandy path toward the water.

When they reached the river, William splashed cool water on his face. It felt so refreshing that he poured a handful over his head as well. He noticed something odd in the water. A person—no, a reflection of someone he hadn't seen in a long, long time.

It was an image of Mrs. Hale when she had spoken to him at the funeral for her son, Jeremy. William quickly looked over his shoulder, expecting to see her. She wasn't there. He looked into the river again. The image moved closer to William, and he remembered the comfort from her kiss on his forehead.

"I forgave you, William," the image spoke, "long ago. Now I see Jeremy every day. We are at peace. Where are you?"

In a flash, William woke from his dream. He looked around his familiar prison cell with its sink, bed, and walls. No cool water. No Jackie or Aria.

William felt tremendous grief and despair. He sat on the edge of his bed and buried his face in his hands. His dream had been so real. Arguing with his daughters at the campfire. Hearing Mrs. Hale. He so wanted to return to that dream so he could ask his girls to guide him the rest of the way home. William closed his eyes and desperately struggled to create the scene at the riverbank in his mind again. The images, however, never reappeared.

William pounded his hands on his bed and yelled, "Arg!" He violently knocked over a table that Ora had placed at the end of the bed. A platter of leftovers spilled onto the floor. William shook his fists in the air and screamed again. He turned around and hit his fists on the bed three times. Thump-thump-thump.

Fatigue, an infection in his body, and now utter despair got the best of William. He slowly knelt by his bed and laid his forehead on top of his folded hands.

"God, I can't go on like this," William finally admitted. "Show me a better way, please. Help me to forgive others. Help me to forgive . . . myself. Especially for hurting Jeremy. It truly was an accident. Please," William lifted his head and pleaded, "I want to live."

At that moment, the cinderblock wall of William's prison disappeared. The concrete floor became cream-colored sand. Coconut trees and berry bushes replaced the sink and bed. William flopped onto a red-and-white checkered picnic cloth, just like the one he had given Lindsay as an anniversary present.

Ora, Gauzette, and two other healers rushed to William's side first. As the healers surrounded William with green, blue, gold, and purple lights, Ora spread a shield around them. She didn't want anyone to interrupt their process. William fell into a deep, peaceful sleep.

The healers made high-pitched noises with their whiskers and touched William with their tentacles. His skin glowed, and his laser wounds started to mend. This process lasted twelve minutes, longer than usual since William's untreated injury had made him so sick.

When the healers finished, Gauzette carried William to his hammock. He was still sleeping, so the healers asked everyone to leave him alone until he woke on his own.

Mitushi escorted the kids to the Healing Quadrant so they could be with William. Ora explained to them and the SEALs that William unconsciously had built the prison cell until he was emotionally ready to enter the Healing Quadrant. He had been beside his squad all this time, but his inability to forgive—especially himself—had separated him from everyone else.

"Will . . . will he be okay?" Aria asked the Gallion healers.

Gauzette touched Aria's head with a tentacle tip and replied, "Healthier than ever."

Later that day, the queen returned to the *Rama* from presiding over a sacred ceremony with the Lemurian High Priestess. Arcthena showed her tapes with highlights of the kids mastering their challenges and the healers working on William.

The queen rubbed a tentacle on Arcthena's shoulder and said, "Splendid progress! I took a risk coming to Earth. The SEALs and youngones finally trust us." The queen lowered her voice and slowly stated, "Now there's only one more thing before we meet in person."

Chapter 34
Dorsal Central

A bright light glared in William's face as he opened his eyes. He swore he thought he saw Lindsay's face, so he called her name. She sweetly answered him and held out her hand. William reached for it, but rolled out of his hammock instead. He fell, face first, in the sand of the Healing Quadrant. At that point William realized he had been dreaming.

"Daddy, Daddy!" Aria cried out from the picnic shelter where she and the SEALs had started eating breakfast. She and Jackie dashed to their father and hugged him with all their might. After his healing, he had slept for nearly two days.

William didn't understand why he and his girls were on a beach. At first, he thought it was another dream. Yet, the tart taste of the sand and the warmth from his girls' hugs made the moment so real. William didn't want it to end. He picked up his girls, swung them around in the air, and told them how much he loved them.

Aria adjusted her sunglasses and asked, "How do you feel, Daddy?"

"Fantastic. Like I'm ten years younger. Stronger than I've ever been." William looked at his right thigh where he had been shot. The wound had healed without a scar. "How . . . how did that happen?"

"We'll explain everything, sir," Elizabeth answered. She and the rest of the group had followed Aria and Jackie to greet William. "We have much to discuss. First, sir, come get some breakfast."

Toothpick added, "You'll love the Starbucks ritual, Captain."

William replied, "Great. I'm so hungry!" He turned to his daughters and challenged them to a race. The three of them kicked up their heels and headed for the picnic shelter. Sand flew all over Tommy and the SEALs.

During breakfast, Elizabeth and Dishtowel briefed Bull's-Eye on everything that had transpired since the Gallions teleported the Navy's aqualaports aboard the *Rama*. Aria, Jackie, and Tommy excitedly told William about their challenges. William said very little about his prison cell, far less than what Ora had told the group yesterday. He described the campfire dream in detail, though. For William, that was the turning point of his life.

After a long breakfast, Princess LeSom entered the Healing Quadrant. Aria ran up to her and gave her a big hug. With so much of her attention recently on the challenges and her father, Aria now realized she had missed her favorite Gallion.

Aria cried out, "Galfriend!"

"Humanfriend!" LeSom cheerfully replied. She made the two-finger peace handshake with Aria.

William shook his head. He knew Aria made friends easily, but this went beyond anything he would have dreamt possible.

LeSom announced, "We welcome you to an exclusive view of your Pacific Ocean in Dorsal Central. Follow me, please."

LeSom led the group to the top of the *Rama*. They entered a large room with a curved, clear ceiling.

Colorful fish, eels, sting rays, squids, sharks, and even a dolphin swam overhead. Seaweed swayed through beams of sunlight. Bleeps, gurgles, and splashing noises echoed in Dorsal Central. LeSom explained that sounds from the water soaked through the transparent barrier instead of bouncing off it.

The SEALs and kids stared at the ceiling, saying "ooh" and "aah" every few seconds. For them it was like going to the largest tropical aquarium without the crowds.

LeSom invited the guests to relax on cushy chairs in the center of the room. She touched a light-blue crystal in her right tentacle and called for Forkana. She entered Dorsal Central a few minutes later with her hospitality apprentices.

Forkana bowed and said, "On behalf of Queen Supreme Nashata, I invite you to a tea with Her Majesty in honor of Aria Vanir."

Aria clapped her hands, jumped around, and squealed, "I get to meet the queen! I finally get to meet the queen!"

Forkana continued, "This will be a formal Gallion tea. My apprentices manifested dress uniforms for the SEALs, a suit for Tommy, and gowns for the youngirls. Everyone will want to look their best for Her Majesty."

Jackie huffed and blared, "Nuke the dress!"

"Oh, please Jackie," Aria pleaded. "Wear a dress and behave for me. Please, please, please, please, please, please."

Forkana approached Jackie with her long gown and said, "We incorporated the colors of your school—yellow and blue. We even added a shoulder sash and pouch for your roamer."

Jackie slipped her roamer into the pouch. It fit perfectly. She slowly nodded her head, rolled her eyes, and acted like it was a big deal for her to comply. Really, she felt just a little excited about the new outfit.

"You owe me one," Jackie said to Aria and she took her gown from Forkana.

Forkana turned to Aria and said, "We made a leather belt with purple strips—which match your sunglasses—to hold your Sword of Purity. It will expand as you grow so you can use it your whole life. Your gown was manifested with purple and white silk to match your sword and favorite color."

Aria squealed again when she saw her gown. She put it up to her body and twirled around like she was dancing at a ball.

Forkana gave Tommy a sling for his bow that matched the pouch for his arrows. She also presented him with a light-gray suit fashioned from the latest James Bond movie. William told Tommy he would look dashing in it.

Once everyone had their clothes, Forkana showed them the formal Gallion tea cup. The large, white mug had handles on opposite ends and a small spout to one side. Forkana explained how the queen served tea from her royal pot into her cup, and then she poured from her cup into the next Gallion's cup. That Gallion dispensed tea from his or her cup into the next Gallion's cup and so forth. When everyone had been served a full cup of tea, then everyone drank together. Having two handles and a spout made the process less drippy.

The SEALs looked at each other with puzzled faces. Finally, Elizabeth asked Forkana how tea from one cup could serve a multitude of Gallions. Forkana's whiskers swayed side-to-side as she pondered Elizabeth's question. At first, Forkana couldn't understand why Elizabeth would ask such a silly question. She remembered, centuries ago, when Gallions had also believed in lack.

"It is a matter of infinity and prosperity," Forkana calmly stated. "Just ask the youngones."

Elizabeth turned to Tommy, who smiled and blushed.

"It's about Oneness," Jackie proudly declared. "Gotta learn how to connect. Be a part—"

"Of everything," Tommy blurted. "Starting with your inner connection."

Elizabeth raised her eyebrows. She didn't understand what her son and Jackie had said, but she enjoyed the sense of peace it brought to her heart.

Forkana continued, "The tea begins in two hours, which is high noon in this Earth time zone. We've manifested showers and dressing rooms for everyone over there." Forkana pointed to doors on the left side of the room. "Relax, spend time with your underwater animals, and prepare for the tea. Her Majesty does appreciate promptness."

Chapter 35
Meeting Queen Supreme Nashata

Precisely at twelve o'clock, Forkana and her apprentices returned to Dorsal Central and escorted the humans to Holospace Four. The Gallions had converted it into a replica of the royal ballroom on Vitchera, where Queen Supreme Nashata conducted formal ceremonies. Aria entered first, followed by Jackie, Tommy, William, Dishtowel, Elizabeth, and the other SEALs by rank. One by one, they walked down an aisle covered with a deep red carpet. Aria felt like a movie star.

Three hundred Gallions stood on either side of the red carpet. They bowed their whiskers and quietly watched as the honorees paraded in front of them.

At the queen's request, LeSom's band played music by the Earth's greatest composers: Bach, Beethoven, Mozart, and Sir Elton John. The queen had forbidden LeSom from playing any of Elvis's songs during the procession.

Aria, Jackie, and Tommy climbed steps to reach a platform where the queen, Mitushi, Ora, and LeSom stood. LeSom's band played on a smaller stage to the right. The three kids stood before the queen, with Aria in the center.

A thin crown of turquoise and amber lights surrounded the queen's whiskers. Jewels that sparked like stars covered her tentacle tips. To Aria, Queen Nashata's skin glowed more brightly than any other Gallion's.

Aria thought about the fabulous events of the past few weeks. Visions of Vitchera, being beamed aboard the *Rama*, her sword, and the challenges. Seeking the Gallion queen had led her on the most auspicious journey of her life.

"On this day," Queen Supreme Nashata began, "we pay homage to Aria Vanir, the Earth youngirl who invited us to visit her home world. She has shown us kindness, friendship, joy, trust, and love. Miss Aria, please step forward."

Aria's eyes widened as she eagerly took two steps toward the queen. Her face beamed with joy and excitement.

The queen said, "There is one, absent, who wishes to be here with you now. She gave you birth and taught you unconditional love in the first memorable moment of your life." The queen turned to Mitushi, who touched a light-blue crystal in his right tentacle to signal First Teleporter Marta.

White lights surrounded Lindsay in the War Plans Room, where she was watching the ceremony on the TV with military officials. In a flash, Marta teleported Lindsay to the ceremony, right beside Aria. Mother and daughter eagerly hugged each other. Tightly.

"I missed you, Mom," Aria admitted. "Now that you're here, everything's astro."

"Thank you," Lindsay politely said to the queen. "You've made a mother's dream come true."

"Yes, I know," the queen responded. "I consider myself to be the mother of all the Gallions in our land. How could I deny you your wish?"

Lindsay gave Jackie a big hug and thanked her for watching over Aria. Forkana escorted Lindsay from the stage to where William was standing. William and Lindsay ran toward each other, embraced, and kissed. The crowd cheered. Lindsay wept again, this time for joy.

"Now that we are all here," the queen continued, "I wish to pay a special tribute to Aria." The queen looked into Aria's blue eyes and declared, "Your extraordinary gifts of distant vision and empathic impression have brought friendship between our worlds. Gallions and humans have coexisted peacefully for several days. With your leadership, Aria, may our friendship extend for generations. You've taught peace to military leaders trained for war and domination. You've shown openness and trust where others claim fear. You've faced repressed rage to master unconditional love. You've raised your Sword of Purity and shown it to those who knew only darkness. For this, I give you a key to the Gallion land, our Pendant of One Hundred Faces."

The Gallions softly made ooh and aah sounds. Their queen entrusted only the most sacred leaders with a key to their land.

Mitushi brought a purple pillow to his mother. On it laid a silvery necklace with a multifaceted pendant. The queen carefully placed the necklace on Aria.

Aria lifted the sparkly pendant to her eyes and stared inside it. She saw images of small mountains, unicorns, and blackbirds diving into a milky ocean. The scenes changed, and Aria witnessed Gallion youngones playing in their homes and grown-up Gallions feeding their communicorns.

Aria turned to face the queen and exclaimed, "It's your land! I see so much of your world through such a small space."

"Size doesn't matter," the queen explained. "Look at all the lives you've touched." Aria turned around to see hundreds of aliens and the SEALs who had considered destroying them. Now, they called themselves friends.

The queen continued, "Use the pendant to view me or other Gallions at any time. Of all the life-forms on Earth, Aria, you are the Gallions' best friend." Then the queen raised all her tentacles and proclaimed, "Cheers!"

"Cheers!" everyone shouted. The audience applauded Aria and chanted her name. She felt like a queen herself.

Meanwhile, Ora stepped forward with a long white pillow that carried two medals of white light. They looked like large Olympic medals, only the ribbons were gold and sparkly.

When the crowd calmed down, the queen called forth Jackie and said, "We honor you, Jacqueline Vanir, for your courage to master the challenge of prosperity. May you connect peacefully with all those you meet, human or alien. We consider you a friend and award you with our Gallion Medal of Spirit." The queen placed one of the medals around Jackie's neck. She again raised her tentacles and yelled, "Cheers!"

The crowd applauded and cheered for Jackie. She clasped her hands together and raised them over her head as though she had won an Olympic medal.

Then the queen called forth Tommy and said, "Thomas Manger, you've shown great inner strength to master the challenge of infinity. May your words continue to proclaim the truth of your existence to all you meet, human or alien. As our friend, I honor you with our Gallion Medal of Spirit." The queen placed the second medal around Tommy's neck and shouted, "Cheers!"

The audience yelled for joy to honor Aria, Jackie, and Tommy. Everyone hugged each other and chatted about the awards. Meanwhile, dozens of hospitality apprentices swiftly distributed the formal Gallion tea cups and set up for the ceremony. When everything was ready, the queen signaled LeSom to start the music. Her band played a tranquil Bach concerto that quieted the crowd.

Queen Supreme Nashata silently poured tea from a large, silvery vessel into her tea cup. Holding onto both handles, she poured tea from her cup into LeSom's. The princess poured tea into Mitushi's cup, and he gave from his cup to Ora's.

Next the queen poured tea from her cup into Aria's cup. Aria watched very, very carefully. The liquid from the queen's cup actually expanded into Aria's cup instead of emptying into it. The drink had multiplied!

Aria whispered, "Just go with it," as she poured tea from her cup into Jackie's and Tommy's.

Jackie went to the first person in the front row to the left of the red carpet, and Tommy did the same on the right. Jackie poured her tea from her cup into her father's, and Tommy into his mother's. William and Elizabeth gave tea from their cup to the SEAL beside them as well as to the Gallion behind them in the second row.

Since the Gallions had been through this ceremony many times, they quickly shared their tea from the second row to the back. When everyone had tea, the queen signaled for the band to stop. The musicians ceased playing and received tea from LeSom's cup.

The queen lifted her cup high above her whiskers and proclaimed, "A toast to friendship, love, prosperity, and infinity. To being connected within and with all. To the Creator who brought us all together. To wholeness!"

"To wholeness!" everyone said in unison. Humans and Gallions clicked cups with their neighbors and repeated, "To wholeness. To wholeness."

First the queen sipped from her cup, with two tentacles extended into the air. The other Gallions followed her lead. The humans sipped their tea and marveled at its delicious, unique flavor.

"Must have a hint of orange mint," Lindsay insisted.

"Chocolate's my guess," Elizabeth countered. "These aliens put chocolate in everything."

"You're both wrong," William demanded. "Blueberry. Definitely blueberry."

"How'd they get this tea to smell like beef jerky?" Tommy wondered.

"Dude, it's banana split," Jackie sarcastically replied.

Aria sniffed her tea and sighed, "Ah, jasmine. I love jasmine."

The queen softly replied, "Yes, I know."

LeSom and the band members guzzled their tea as gracefully as possible. They needed to scurry backstage and change for the next part of the ceremony.

When everyone had finished with their tea, Forkana and Peakte transformed the red-carpet ceremonial ballroom into a huge dance floor. They dimmed the lights and lowered shiny balls from the ceilings.

"Oh, no," William said to Lindsay. "This looks like the 1970s. At least from what I've seen in those dance movies and pictures of my grandparents."

The hospitality apprentices politely ushered everyone except the queen from the platform. They hung black curtains for the next part of the ceremony. When they finished, the queen raised her tentacles to quiet the crowd.

"I'm so glad to see you, William," Lindsay whispered to her husband. She kissed her husband's clean, just-shaven face. "I've been watching everything from—"

The queen spoke, "My sister has planned a splendid surprise for our young guests. She told me they'd love it, and I would probably go nuclear." The audience chuckled. "So Gallions and human friends, give a warm *Rama* welcome to Princess LeSom and the Elvins!"

The curtains opened. Princess LeSom, cloaked in a blue velvet cape, strolled to the front of the stage. She somberly looked over the audience as her drummer started a slow, you-know-something's-coming beat. LeSom lifted her head. She passionately flung off her cape to expose her body in a black leather suit and a three-necked guitar in her tentacles.

LeSom yelled at the top of her lungs, "Let's rock the *Rama*!" Her tentacles flew up and down the necks of her guitar to generate a sound that would make the most famous rock star envious.

The crowd went wild! The curtain was drawn back to show LeSom's new revorock band members, who were also dressed in skintight leather outfits. The drummer even had a colorful tattoo on his right tentacle.

LeSom pranced around the stage and sang, "I'm beaming up so you better get this party started." She thought a modern remake of Pink's "Get the Party Started" would put everyone in a dancing frame of mind. Oh, was she right.

The kids ran up to the edge of the stage, screaming and waving their arms to get a touch of LeSom's tentacles. They felt like they were standing front-row at a real rock concert. Within seconds, the performance became the best part of their adventures with the Gallions.

Humans and Gallions started to boogie down. Tentacles wiggled everywhere, hips gyrated, and whiskers bounced with the beat of the band. Guys twirled the ladies. Women flaunted their curves. Even the queen shook her groove thing.

"How'd they find out about our music?" Lindsay shouted to Elizabeth.

"They know everything about us," Elizabeth yelled into Lindsay's ear. "Wait until you see Starbucks in the morning."

LeSom and her band had downloaded Aria's "My Favorites" from her tMuz into their whiskers. They watched music videos from the tMuz and Gallery of Worlds. The music and steps weren't that difficult for them to learn in a few hours. Getting fitted for the skintight leather suits took forever.

As LeSom and the Elvins played hit after hit, the hospitality apprentices set up a waterfall and large, smooth rocks where worn-out dancers could relax. At Ringer's request, they even manifested their chocolate-filled coconuts for an after-tea delight.

For the first song after a break, LeSom changed her voice to an English accent and announced, "Me and the band wrote this next song, and we want to dedicate it to Aria. It's called 'Make the Nights Bright.' It's a slow one, so pick a partner who won't step all over your tentacles."

For a moment, Aria waited to see if Tommy would ask her to dance. Then she changed her mind. She walked over to her father, who was sitting on a rock with Lindsay by the waterfall, and asked him instead. William beamed with pride.

"Enjoy it now," Lindsay said to her husband as he left with Aria. "In a few years she'll be embarrassed by everything you do."

The queen's whiskers parted into a U as she listened to the unusually soothing song and watched Aria dance with her handsome father. The queen stretched her tentacles seven feet to touch Mitushi. He walked to her side and asked her to dance.

"Thank you for bringing me here," the queen said to her son. "Our mission has been quite successful."

"All because you had the courage to trust one youngirl, Mother."

The queen replied, "All because she had the courage to trust an alien message."

"I'm very proud of you," William said to Aria during their dance. "No other father has a daughter with the key to the Gallion land."

"Yeah, that's astro," Aria admitted. "Somehow I just knew we had friends among the stars."

Chapter 36
Aria's Assignment

Early the next morning, Queen Supreme Nashata asked Forkana to invite Jackie, Aria, and Tommy to the royal suite for breakfast with Her Majesty. The queen wanted to spend some quality time with the youngirls and younguy before the Gallions departed Earth. Something about their excitement and awe of life reminded the queen of youngones on Vitchera. Perhaps they weren't so different after all.

During breakfast the kids asked question after question about the Gallion land on Vitchera.

"How large is your country?"

"How many Gallions live there?"

"Do leaves drop off the trees in fall?

"Does it snow there?"

"How high do the waves get?"

"Do you celebrate Christmas or Hanukkah?"

"Are you married to a king?"

Soon the queen realized another similarity between youngones of Vitchera and Earth: Curiosity. She patiently answered all their questions and even showed them images of the Gallion land in her viewing room.

The wise queen had discovered from years of diplomatic adventures that species who learned and laughed together rarely fought with each other. She wanted to make a grand impression on the youngones that they would remember for the rest of their lives and eagerly share with others. The spark of friendship that had ignited with this journey would, hopefully, spread like wildfire through other human hearts.

"I have duties for you," the queen announced after an hour of answering questions.

Tommy sheepishly asked, "Chores?" He hoped he didn't have to vacuum anything.

"More like . . . responsibilities," the queen explained. "First, use your gifts. They chose you for a reason. Practice with them daily, even just for twenty minutes, to become proficient. Second, I want each of you to serve as honorary ambassadors between our countries. Tommy, be strong and bold when people ask you about these aliens called Gallions. Jackie, remember to connect with others before you tell them about your adventures on the *Rama*. They will be far more likely to trust you. And Aria, I have a special assignment for you."

The queen tapped a light-blue crystal on her right tentacle and told Peakte she was ready. He arrived a minute later with Aria's tDiary.

"My tDiary!" Aria exclaimed. "Did you fix it?"

"Indeed, indeed," Peakte answered. "Plus modifications."

"Modifications?" Aria asked.

"Indeed, indeed. I added a retinal scan so your sister can't access the tDiary without your being present. Try it."

"That was my request," the queen added, glaring at Jackie.

Aria placed the tDiary on a table and lifted its lid. A beam automatically scanned her face. The following phrase displayed on the screen: "Retinal scan passed. Press tScan and enter password."

"The really nifty part is this extra key I added." Peakte pointed to a purple button labeled *Gal*. Aria, Jackie, and Tommy bumped heads as they all looked at the keyboard.

"What does it do?" Aria inquired.

The queen suggested, "Press it and find out. However, I advise you and the others to first take a step back."

Aria leaned away from the tDiary. Jackie and Tommy stood behind her and peered over her shoulders.

Then Aria muttered, "Here it goes," and pressed the purple button. A beam of light flashed upward from the Gallion button. Holographic images appeared three feet above the tDiary.

"Astro!" Tommy exclaimed. He and Jackie pressed against Aria's back to get a closer look at the images.

"Recognize the scenes, Aria?" the queen inquired.

"Definitely. It's like a movie of what's happened to me since I was beamed up."

"With enhanced video and audio," Peakte added. He pointed to the side of the tDiary and explained, "Slide your tentacles—I mean, fingers—here to modify picture and speakers."

Aria adjusted the images until they came into sharper focus than the tHTV at home. Surround sound blared from the speakers.

"Astro fizz!" Aria yelled over the people talking in the images from her tDiary. She turned down the volume and watched the scenes for several minutes.

The queen explained, "Consider it a documentary of your adventures with the Gallions. Arcthena downloaded favorite features from her observations of your family and the American government. We also established a transmission link from your sunglasses to our ship's crystal recorder and from there to your tDiary. Everything you saw, everything said to you, everything you said, and all your reactions were captured and stored for historical purposes."

Aria whispered into the queen's whiskers, "Even when I went to the bathroom?"

The queen shook her head and replied, "Certainly not. Arcthena turned off the transmissions during any . . . times of privacy."

Jackie turned to her sister and said, "Talk about a galactic reality show."

"More importantly," the queen continued, "we created a transmission link from Aria's glasses to a rectangular communication device at your father's naval air station."

"Plasma television," Peakte clarified.

The queen replied, "Yes, thank you. That way your government and military could witness your experiences and learn about the Gallions from your perspective. When attempts at peaceful negations with your father's SEAL squad failed, we needed a way to communicate our sincere interest in friendship to your leaders. We decided to allow your eyes, Aria, communicate this vital message."

"Why didn't you tell me?" Aria whined. "I feel a little . . . weird. I mean, like, everything I said was taped. Isn't that like Watergate?"

"If you had known, Aria, your actions and responses wouldn't have been genuine. This way, the people of Earth will know the truth about the Gallions from our best humanfriend. Aria, you are our hero."

The queen and other Gallions in the royal suite bowed their heads to Aria. She blushed and lowered her head in return.

"I get it now," Aria said to the queen. "You needed someone you trusted to gather top-secret intel and relay that information on a need-to-know basis to the proper authorities."

Jackie patted her sister on the back as she said, "You're getting the hang of this spy business."

Tommy bumped shoulders with Aria and said, "Dude, you're famous!"

Aria whispered to him, "I just hope they weren't listening when I sang with Princess LeSom."

The queen added, "Also, your mother started watching soon after we beamed Jackie and Tommy aboard. All the history is there, in your tDiary. Just say 'menu' to select scenes based on category or date."

Aria called out, "Menu."

In a feminine voice, the tDiary asked, "Would you like to review scenes based on person, topic, or date?"

"My tDiary's never talked like that. Ever!"

"Indeed, indeed," Peakte replied. "It's a modification."

"Astro!" Aria exclaimed as she poked her fingers through the holograms. She paused to think about what she wanted to view. "Person. Mom. I mean, Lindsay Vanir."

Scenes of Lindsay appeared. Beating up the MPs. Cheering during her daughters' challenges. Jumping for joy when William was healed. Being teleported to the *Rama*. Aria and Jackie watched with great interest. They gained a new perspective on their mother.

The queen explained, "Peakte wrote an instruction crystal on the new features of your tDiary. LeSom translated it into American teen slang. Just in case something isn't clear, I want you to spend as much time as needed with Peakte to learn all the modifications and new controls. Oh and Aria, we'll download periodic upgrades free of charge."

Aria giggled. The queen reminded her of her math teacher. Nice, but always so serious.

"Your sunglasses," the queen continued, "will transmit to our crystal record for as long as you wish. Whenever you want to show us something or speak to us, simply put on your sunglasses."

"How will I hear from you?" Aria asked.

The queen answered, "Your tDiary has a special slot for the pendant I gave you yesterday. Peakte, please show her." Peakte pointed one of his tentacle tips to a new opening in the front of Aria's tDiary. "Your pendant will glow green when we have a message for you. Simply slip the pendant in that slot, and our communication will be transmitted to you. It's all in the instruction crystal."

Aria took a deep breath. She felt overwhelmed by all the new gadgets.

The queen looked Aria in the eyes and stated, "So your mission, should you agree to take it, is to show this documentary of your adventures with the Gallions to the right people at the right time in the right way. We want our messages of friendship, love, prosperity, and infinity to spread to all humans. For that, we trust your insights."

Aria wrinkled her forehead and moaned, "How will I know what to do? I'm only twelve years old. I'm not even in high school yet. Shouldn't I have a college degree first?"

The queen leaned closer to Aria and responded, "Ask your Sword of Purity and trust its guidance. It lights your path of destiny." Then the queen placed her tentacle tips on Aria's shoulders and stated, "Humans are at the brink of a conscious evolution. They must decide whether to continue with the old ways of war and domination or accept new ways of love, prosperity, and infinity. We want humans to move forward in their destiny. That is why we are here, today, with you."

Silence filled the royal suite. Aria didn't quite understand the concept of a conscious evolution. She figured it had to do with the challenges she had faced with Jackie, Tommy, and her father. Perhaps others will experience similar struggles, Aria assumed. If so, she believed the lessons from the Gallions would inspire them to make decisions for their highest good.

With that in mind, Aria got it. She felt excited about this destiny.

Aria straightened her shoulders, looked the queen in the eyes, and declared, "Yes! Yes, I accept the mission!"

The queen joyfully replied, "Splendid! Now there's one more thing I need to do. Aria, look at me for a moment." Aria turned to the queen. Her Majesty adjusted Aria's glasses to ensure they were working properly. The queen turned to Jackie and quietly asked, "How do I look?"

Jackie smiled and replied, "Spicy splash, your majesty."

So the queen looked into Aria's sunglasses again and said, "To the military personnel in Virginia Beach. This marks the end of our transmissions. General Goforth, Vice Admiral Jennings, and the rest of you—your records of us will be deleted. Aria is now responsible for the Gallion documentary." The queen's whiskers fanned out as she firmly warned, "If you tamper with her tDiary, touch one whisker—I mean hair—on her head, or attempt to take away any of the gifts we've given to the youngones, you will feel my wrath!"

The queen signaled to Peakte to cease the transmissions to Virginia Beach. He touched a black crystal attached to his right tentacle and then nodded to the queen.

"Destroy all their knowledge of us," the queen ordered to Peakte. "Leave no trace of Aria and the Gallions in their tapes, papers, and any other primitive technology they are using."

"With pleasure," Peakte said as he tapped gray and red crystals on his tentacles.

The queen added, "Do your best not to injure any of the humans. They can keep their memories of us. This time."

Chapter 37
Returning Home

While the queen spent the day with the youngsters, Mitushi gave the SEALs and Lindsay a tour of the *Rama*. He and his crew attempted to answer their questions about biomolecular transformation, vibrational healing, free energy propulsion, and altability. However, each answer led to even more questions.

"We'll get there someday," William told Mitushi as they toured Central Control. "I see now why Aria trusted you so much. Commander Supreme, I . . . I apologize for attacking you and your crew. I accept full responsibility for the consequences."

Mitushi quickly replied, "Yes, Captain, you have taken responsibility for the consequences. You've learned to forgive and to be forgiven. We are friends now, not enemies."

"Friends."

"One day," Mitushi continued, "you will learn we are all one."

At the end of the day, the humans, the royal family, and the Gallion first officers gathered in Holospace Two. The Gallions had repaired the SEALs' aqualaports, and it was time to leave. Humans and aliens hugged, gave the two-finger peace handshake, and said final good-byes. Everyone departed on friendly terms. The diplomatic journey had been galactically successful.

The queen said to William, "You and your family are welcome to visit my palace anytime. Think about it for your Christmas vacation."

Aria tugged on her father's uniform and pleaded, "Oh, can we, please? Please, please, please, please, please."

"You'll need an intergalactic passport," the queen explained to William. "So make sure everyone has a recent photo. Oh, one other thing—you can't take poppy seeds through wormhole customs."

The Gallions teleported Lindsay, Jackie, Aria, and Tommy to their homes. William ordered the SEALs to prepare their aqualaports for departure.

"By the way," Peakte quickly said to William. "Don't be surprised if the propulsion exceeds original parameters. We made a few . . . modifications."

"Thanks," William replied. "I think." He turned to Mitushi and asked, "Will you return to Vitchera now?"

"Not yet. First we plan to take several days to observe your whales and dolphins. We're fascinated by their sounds. LeSom says she wants to play some of her original music for them. Gauzette believes our healers can soothe the injuries they've suffered from sonar experiments. We've learned to use vibrations in ways that cause no harm to creatures around us."

"Commander Supreme, come with me—as my guest. Meet the President of the United States. Teach us about healing, not harming, the whales and dolphins. Visit with ambassadors from all over Earth. Get on CNN. Sure will make my briefings more believable if you're there."

"Thanks, but that's not my mission. I'm sure you can handle your briefings without me. They may not believe you, Captain Vanir, but they will notice something shiny about you. People will talk about how much you and your crew have changed—in a positive way."

William smiled and gave a thumbs-up signal. Mitushi raised two tentacle tips to form a peace sign. Once opposing warriors, they had become friends.

Later that summer, Aria sat at her desk and gazed at the sky to watch the first stars appear. As she tapped her fingers on the top of her tDiary, she noticed a flashing green light in her bedroom window. It was a reflection of the Gallion Pendant of One Hundred Faces she was wearing. The Gallions were sending her a message!

Aria hastily opened her tDiary and placed her pendant into its special slot. The tDiary instantly projected an image of Queen Supreme Nashata. Aria wondered what adventure awaited her now.

75035197R00138

Made in the USA
Columbia, SC
16 September 2019